FIRST IMPRESSIONS

FIVE SHORT LOVE STORIES

KATE COURTRIGHT

WILD WATER PRESS

Published in 2023 by Wild Water Press, LLC
Copyright 2023 by Kate Courtright
Cover Design and Illustrations: MaryDes, marydes.eu
EBook ISBN: 978-1-959491-00-2
Paperback ISBN: 978-1-959-491-01-9
Hardcover ISBN: 978-1-959491-02-6

These short stories and novellas are original works of fiction. Names,
characters, places, and incidents are the products of the author's imagination or
are used fictitiously. Any resemblance to actual events, organizations, locales, or
persons, living or dead, is entirely coincidental.

This book is dedicated in loving memory to my cousin and writing role model, Elisabeth Stevens.

ABOUT THESE FIVE SHORT LOVE STORIES

PINKIE: Rebecca returns her ex's diamond ring, then boards a train in wintry Utica, New York, determined that next time around, she'll take her time getting to know a man before making any kind of romantic commitment.

FORMER THINGS: Just as his beloved grandmother's funeral begins, a woman Sean never expected to lay eyes on again walks into the sanctuary.

IT'S UP TO YOU, NEW YORK: A Wisconsin empty nester moves to NYC hoping it's not too late to embark on a new chapter in this city of dreams.

FIRE BOY: More than ready for a fresh start after her broken engagement, Heidi arrives at an old-fashioned Adirondack resort one dark and stormy night and starts right off on the wrong foot with the resort's brooding "fire boy."

CHEMISTRY LESSONS: Recent divorcee Gretchen attends her thirtieth high school reunion looking forward to fun with old friends, not to having her world turned upside down by a completely unexpected blast from the past.

Whether recovering from betrayal, heartbreak, bad choices, or just the fact that life can be so difficult, the characters in these short stories and novellas must choose whether to play it safe or dare to risk their vulnerable hearts one more time.

CONTENTS

PINKIE

FORMER THINGS

IT'S UP TO YOU, NEW YORK

FIRE BOY

CHEMISTRY LESSONS

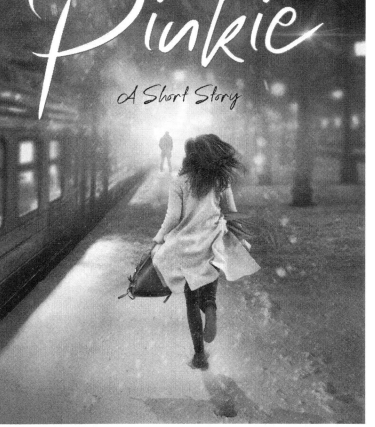

1

UTICA

"Not Windex," Rebecca insisted, pulling her hand away from her mother-in-law's—her ex-mother-in-law's—clutches.

Tabitha held the squirt bottle menacingly and stared at the diamond ring on Rebecca's finger with covetous longing.

"It works," Tabitha said.

"I don't care. I'm serious, Tabitha. Don't spray that stuff on me."

Tabitha raised her stony gray eyes and said, "Olive oil, then." She flung the Windex bottle onto the linoleum counter where it skittered into a plastic dish drainer, knocking a colander into the sink.

The woman's intense focus alarmed Rebecca, who pulled again on the diamond ring, wanting it off, off, off. It was no use. The knuckle on her finger had swollen, and the ring she wanted so desperately to return to its original family seemed determined to burrow into her flesh.

"Why you're still wearing that is beyond me." Tabitha grasped Rebecca's wrist and extended her hand above the sink, liberally dousing her fingers with olive oil. "The divorce came through weeks ago. Second thoughts?"

"No!" Rebecca cried. "I just didn't want to lose it. I know how important this ring is to all of you and I wanted to make sure I returned it safely." She wanted to make sure her husband's—her ex-husband's family—had nothing to hold over her head. She'd come all the way from her new home in Richmond, Virginia, back to Utica, New York, to spend one more night at this ranch house on Dwyer Street. She'd lived for two miserable years under her mother-in-law's roof before she'd left Kenny. Now she had only to hand this ring over to the woman to be done with this whole sad episode of her life once and for all.

And she had one more suitcase of belongings that Tabitha had insisted she retrieve in person, even though Rebecca had urged her to just throw all her things out. She was grateful Tabitha hadn't listened to her. Somehow, the woman had known she would want her stuffed pink rabbit, Igloo, and a few other mementos from her childhood. There was kindness under that gruff exterior.

She had hoped to at least say goodbye to Kenny. But the whole twenty-four hours she'd been here, Kenny had not emerged from his room. He was probably playing video games, his favorite evening and weekend activity, for as long as she'd known him. She had married a twenty-six-year-old boy and divorced a twenty-eight-year-old boy, who seemed to think that becoming a controlling jerk made him into a man.

"There!" Tabitha cried.

The ring slipped off her finger so quickly and Tabitha thrust her hand away with so much force that Rebecca lost her balance, and collided pinkie first with the cupboard door. She stood, stupidly, staring at her finger, which now jutted at a revolting right angle away from the others on her hand. She didn't know if it was the sight of the mutilated appendage or the sudden, harrowing pain that brought on the nausea, but the next moment she was leaning over the sink, puking into the colander.

"Oh, for Pete's sake, what have you done now?" Tabitha snapped.

Mutely, Rebecca raised her hand, pointer finger toward the ceiling, pinkie finger pointing accusingly at her mother-in-law. Her ex-mother-law.

"Oh." Tabitha placed the diamond ring on the spice rack beside the paprika and wiped the olive oil off her fingers with a paper towel.

Rebecca sat abruptly on a stool, a foul taste in her mouth. She really should run the water in the kitchen sink, get that nastiness out of the colander and down the drain. She couldn't make herself stand up. "I have to catch my train," she said.

"You need to change your reservation," Tabitha said. "Kenny!" she called down the hall. "I have to get to my poker game. Can you please take Rebecca to the emergency room? She's broken her finger."

A moment of silence followed. The two women looked at each other, waiting.

"She's not my wife anymore," Kenny called back. "She doesn't want to take care of me, and I don't have to take care of her."

Even through her pain, Rebecca heard the hurt in her ex-husband's voice, and felt for him. Still. What an asshole. *You never did take care of me!* she felt like shouting. He milked every illness and injury he had for all it was worth, but he had no patience with any complaint of hers. He resented her student loans and repeatedly implied that she had not been transparent about how much debt she was bringing into their relationship, which was patently untrue.

And never had he lifted a finger to do anything—laundry,

shopping, cooking, cleaning, yard work—that his mother or Rebecca could do instead, rationalizing that since he earned more money than both of them with his construction job, he shouldn't have to, even though they both worked longer hours at the bank. When he started using "head of the household" language and determining where every cent of her paycheck needed to go (except for what he considered a reasonable allowance) all while making no effort to create a separate household for the two of them, she'd had enough. The little voice in her head saying *Get out now!* had grown from a whisper to a shout, and she had listened.

For once, Tabitha had the courtesy to look slightly mortified, offering just a hint of acknowledgement that this man's upbringing might be somewhat to blame for the selfishness, bossiness, and downright laziness he perpetually displayed. And looking into her ex-mother-in-law's tired gray eyes, with the crow's feet, and dark bags underneath, Rebecca felt a greater tinge of sympathy than she had previously known. Kenny was his own person. The failure of their marriage was not this woman's fault. Rebecca never should have agreed to live with Tabitha in the first place. If her own parents hadn't moved to Florida, leaving her essentially homeless; if she and Kenny had waited to marry till they could afford their own place instead of her moving in with Kenny and Tabitha; if she'd had any confidence that she might be able to support herself for a bit before plunging into marriage—maybe she wouldn't be in this painful situation right now.

If, if, if. It didn't matter. The marriage was over.

Tabitha reached for her coat and car keys and draped Rebecca's winter coat over her shoulders. "I'm going to have to drop you at the station after we get your finger taken care of. You might have a long wait for your train."

"I'm sorry," Rebecca said. "I hate to make you miss your

game." This weekly gathering of old friends was one of the few leisure activities in Tabitha's life, and Rebecca truly was sorry to interfere with it.

"Well." Tabitha looked dubiously at Rebecca's mutilated hand. "Don't mind that."

"Mom!" Kenny called from down the hall. "We're out of cereal."

Rebecca tried hard to stifle a sigh. Fortunately, the throbbing pain kept her focused.

"Kenny, come say goodbye to Rebecca," his mother scolded.

"I already said goodbye to her."

Tabitha walked out the door, shrugging.

Rebecca paused on the threshold. "'Bye, Kenny," she called out, feeling unexpectedly charitable. He was stuck with himself, but she was free. Free. "Don't worry about me. I'm fine."

Silence answered her. She followed Tabitha out the side door to the driveway, gingerly holding her hand.

Three hours, one emergency room visit, and one enormous cast on her smallest finger later, Rebecca leaned over in the car and gave her ex-mother-in-law a kiss on the cheek.

"Thank you for everything."

"Drop a note once in a while," the older woman said gruffly.

Rebecca forced a sad smile. Of everything she was leaving behind, this brusque but dependable woman might be the only thing she would actually miss a little. "I will."

She exited the car, pulled the bulky, wheel-less suitcase out of the trunk with her good hand, and waved goodbye. Dragging the suitcase through the double doors and across the floor of Utica's majestic train station turned into an athletic event. When she finally reached the smooth wooden bench closest to the ticket window, she was damp with perspiration. Shrugging off her winter coat, she draped it over her suitcase and went to inquire about the train's ETA, keeping a careful eye on her possessions, although she doubted anyone would be tempted to abscond with her bulky luggage. Amazingly, she hadn't missed her train. It was running very late because of snow on the tracks in Rochester, the clerk informed her.

Tired as she was, the pain in her finger kept her from falling asleep on the bench. It throbbed, keeping time with her heartbeat. She was astonished to discover in the last few hours just how much she used her left hand, now that it could barely function. To make matters worse, it looked ridiculous. It seemed that everyone who passed her on the way to the ticket window cast a side glance at the mummified sausage that was her poor, broken finger.

Oh well. What use was vanity at a time like this? In that sensible frame of mind, she removed her contact lenses to give her dry eyes a rest and put on her glasses. She didn't like how she looked in glasses, but it's not like she would see anyone she knew on this train ride. She planned to sleep nonstop till she got home.

2

ALBANY

Two hours later, she followed her fellow travelers out to the track, dragging her unwieldy suitcase behind her. Her shoulders ached. Her finger throbbed. Thankfully, the conductor lifted the suitcase onto the train for her, but she still had to lug it down the aisle while she searched for an empty seat. An announcement over the loudspeaker warned that the train was sold out and every available seat must be used. She reached the end of the compartment before she found one aisle seat, unoccupied except for a backpack. A man sprawled on the companion seat, face pressed against the window, gently snoring.

"Excuse me," Rebecca said. The man didn't move. "Excuse me," she said again. He snored more loudly. Her patience ran out and though she honestly meant to just nudge his leg with her toe, her irritation added a little oomph and it ended up being more like a kick.

"What the hell?" the man said, jerking awake, brushing his mop of brown hair away from his forehead. He looked at her with confusion, then down at her sausage finger, then at the empty seat beside him. "Oh, gosh, I'm sorry. Here." He moved the backpack to the floor by his feet.

"Thank you." She scanned the overhead racks but could see no empty pockets of space for her suitcase. A woman behind her cleared her throat and Rebecca realized she was holding up a line of people who needed to get through to the next car to continue their search for unoccupied seats. Hoisting the suitcase onto her seat, she pressed away from the aisle to let her fellow passengers by. Great. She'd found a seat, but her suitcase might need it, so she might have to stand the whole way to Virginia, she thought morosely. Even though she knew she was imagining the worst and feeling embarrassingly sorry for herself, a tear trickled down her cheek.

"Hey, Pinkie, don't cry," the man beside her said gently. "I'll help you."

Rebecca wiped her cheek with the back of her hand, knocking her pinkie cast against her glasses. "Thank you," she sniffled, with as much dignity as she could muster.

As soon as the aisle cleared, she stepped into it. The man, wide awake now and full of energy, stepped out and walked up and down the aisle assessing the overhead rack situation. He then took it upon himself to move people's luggage around to arrange everything more compactly. He had a few inches on her and was wiry, but obviously strong, as these exertions seemed to cost him little effort. A number of people eyed him suspiciously, but no one spoke up in protest. Eventually, he cleared a space large enough to fit her suitcase, which he lifted up as if it were filled only with cotton balls and lodged it securely in place. With a half-bow, he turned to her. "Aisle or window seat, Pinkie?"

Rebecca moved into the window seat, handing the man his backpack. She'd never had a nickname in her life, having been adamant about being called Rebecca, not Becky, since kindergarten. Wouldn't it just serve her right if she ended up with

Pinkie as a nickname—a perpetual reminder of her failure in love?

"I know it's none of my business," the man said, revealing a subtle Southern drawl as he settled into the chair beside her and gestured to her hand, "but I'm curious. What'd you do?" He had warm brown eyes and locks of brown hair falling over his forehead, almost reaching his thick, dark eyebrows. He definitely needed a haircut. His lips tilted down, giving the impression that he was granting serious thought to the question. A white scar ran from his lower lip half an inch down his chin.

"Oh, it was stupid. I was too vigorous in taking off my diamond ring."

He looked startled. "You were engaged?"

"No, married. I mean, I was married. I'm not anymore. I'm divorced. And I've given back the family's engagement ring, and this is my reward: a broken finger."

"Oh." He pondered this. A twinkle in his eye belied the otherwise solemn expression on his face. "So, are congratulations or condolences in order?"

She hesitated a moment. "It's just sad," and then added, "I really don't want to talk about it," in a tone that she meant to be off-putting. She did not want to talk about the dissolution of her marriage. Not at all. But feeling regret over her sharp tone, she added, "I'm sorry. I'm just tired."

"Well, I guess it is midnight," he said, looking slightly disappointed. "I was conked out before, but I'm wide awake now. Don't worry. I'll be quiet."

Rebecca arranged her coat into a pillow, reclined her seat as far as it would go, and turned away from her companion. The gentle lull of the train's movement soothed her to a semblance of sleep. Hours passed. She was vaguely aware of passengers exiting or boarding the train. For a time, she shivered with cold, but then she began to feel warm, as if a blanket covered her.

During intermittent moments of consciousness, she fell into that welcome reverie prompted by long train rides. What a welcome respite from life this train ride was, an interim time and space between the bitterness of marital failure behind her and the daunting hurdles ahead of her. It was harder than she thought it would be: trying to establish herself in a new city where she was a complete unknown. She'd been in Richmond four months now, and though she had plenty of friendly interactions with people, she had yet to make a real friend. Sleep, she reminded herself, fretfully. Sleep. She slept.

She felt toasty warm, and surprisingly comfortable, until the throbbing in her finger finally forced her to wake, at which point she realized she was leaning heavily against her companion, resting her head on his shoulder. She opened her eyes and sat bolt upright. How mortifying. What must he think of her? What if she'd drooled on him? Why had he tolerated that total intrusion into his physical space? She couldn't look at him. Her cheeks flamed with heat.

The train had stopped. Nothing but darkness appeared out the window. She took a quick glance to her left. Her companion sat, eyes on his e-reader, pretending to be oblivious to the fact that she had just removed her head from his shoulder. She tugged the blanket closer to her neck and looked out the window again, then back at the man beside her. She would pretend she had no idea what she'd done in her sleep.

"Are we almost at Penn Station?"

He shook his head. "We're stuck about two miles outside of Albany."

"Albany!" she cried.

"Shhh!" someone behind her hissed.

"Albany?" she whispered. "I thought I was asleep for hours."

"You were. About five hours," he said quietly.

"Then how can we only be at Albany? That's less than a hundred miles from Utica."

"Well, we obviously haven't been moving very fast. Track trouble. Anxious to get back home?"

"Not really," she admitted. She glanced at her phone. 5:30 a.m. "Well, I guess I missed the connection to Richmond."

"That's where you're headed?"

She nodded. He seemed to be waiting for her to say something. "You?"

"A town that some consider the center of the universe," he said, smiling. "Can you guess?"

She shook her head. She felt curious, but cautious about engaging in even this simple a conversation. She didn't know this person. He seemed perfectly decent, but she had demonstrated well what a poor judge of character she was when it came to men. Not that this man was interested in anything more than being a friendly train acquaintance. He certainly seemed not to want her to be embarrassed about sleeping on his shoulder, and she appreciated that.

The train lurched forward, stopped, lurched again, causing her to bump shoulders twice with her companion. The loudspeaker crackled and the conductor announced that in a few minutes the train would pull into Albany train station for an hour layover while they switched engines. Amtrak guests were free to enter the station for some refreshment if they wished. They apologized for the delays caused by train and track trouble. They hoped to make up the time if they could.

Her finger throbbed.

"You want to get some coffee, Pinkie?" her seatmate asked.

"That's not my name."

"I'd be surprised if it was. I don't know your name, so at this point I don't know what else to call you." Again, that southern drawl, which made his words seem so agreeable.

She hesitated for a moment, then said, "I guess Pinkie's fine for now."

"Who knows? It might stick."

"I would say the odds of that are very low."

He pondered her. "I would say the odds of that are low to fair." He winked.

Her heart fluttered. Oh, for goodness' sake, what was the matter with her? The last thing she wanted to do was engage in some kind of flirtation with a very attractive man, when she was literally only hours away from having left her ex-husband for good. Not to mention, she was wearing her glasses and looking far from her best. He probably wasn't even flirting. He was probably simply being kind to someone who'd just broken her finger and left her husband.

She pulled her bandaged hand from the blanket and stared at it resentfully. Then she looked at the blanket, puzzled. "Where did this come from? I didn't bring a blanket."

"They were giving them out. You were shivering." He shrugged and returned his focus to his e-reader, slightly embarrassed. "I hope you don't mind. It was a little presumptuous of me, I suppose."

She felt touched. What a thoughtful thing to do. "No, I don't mind. Thank you." She pulled out her bottle of pain pills and then put them back in her purse. "I need some water."

The train moved the last couple of miles into Albany, and the doors opened. Her seatmate stepped into the aisle and pulled on his coat. "First stop, water. Second stop, coffee."

She stood, slid her right arm into her coat sleeve, and draped the rest of her coat over her left shoulder. She probably could fit her left hand through the sleeve, but she was afraid the cast might snag along the way. She followed her seatmate off the train, up the stairs and into the station. She wanted to know his name, but she was fairly certain she was going to have to volunteer hers before he shared his, and she felt oddly reluctant to do so.

She purchased a water bottle and swallowed her pain tablets before she even left the store. Then she walked beside him to the coffee shop. "Oh," she said, looking at the display of baked goods. "They sell half-moon cookies here. I love these. I've never seen them anywhere outside of upstate New York."

"Well, I've seen them in Manhattan. They're called black-and-whites there."

She looked at him indignantly. "Black-and-whites bear only a passing resemblance to half-moon cookies. Black-and-whites are a cookie. Half-moon cookies are a cake."

He eyed her solemnly. "Half-moon cookies are a cake," he repeated.

She smiled, hearing how silly that sounded. "Okay, they are cake-like cookies, then. They taste completely different from black-and-whites! I actually get homesick for these."

"Grab us a table. Take anything in your coffee?"

"Just milk. Thanks."

She sat at a small table and draped her coat over the other seat, as the café was starting to get crowded. He appeared a few moments later, carrying a tray with two coffees, a half-moon cookie with extra thick layers of black and white frosting, and a blueberry muffin.

"What do I owe you?"

A stubborn expression flitted across his face, which then relaxed. "How about you get the coffee in Penn Station?"

So, they'd be traveling some distance in the same direction. She relented. "Okay, so, how far is the center of the universe?"

He grinned. "Ashland, Virginia. You never heard it called that?"

She shook her head. "You're going almost as far as I am."

He poured four packets of sugar into his creamy coffee. "Yes. Is Richmond home?"

She blew on her coffee. She had to be careful or before she knew it she'd be blurting out the story of her life to this man, and if he turned out to be as sweet and decent as he appeared so far, she might develop feelings for him, given her vulnerable emotional state. And then he would get off the train in Ashland and she'd never see him again, and she would feel even worse when she got home than she had already anticipated feeling.

"Do I look like a serial killer to you?" he asked.

She shook her head.

"Then why are you so afraid to talk to me?"

Her cheeks grew warm. She blew into her coffee again. "I'm not afraid. I just don't usually talk to strange men."

He leaned back, his handsome face suddenly somber, his brown eyes gazing at her shyly.

"Listen, if you want me to leave you alone, just say so. I don't mean to be intrusive or upset you in any way."

Her pulse quickened with panic. He'd do it: leave her alone, if she asked him to. He'd turn cool and polite and find another seat as soon as he could. She did not want that. She had no idea what she did want, but she did not want him to leave her alone. "No, actually, I don't want that. I'm sorry I'm so awkward. I've never been good at this kind of thing."

"Small talk?" He took a swig of coffee and relaxed his posture.

She nodded.

"Most people aren't. It's getting worse now that we all have these devices." He gestured to the people sitting around them, a dozen or more, all focused intently on their phones. Aside from the two of them, nobody was speaking to anyone else.

"You're right," she agreed, thinking of Kenny, glued to his video games, with no time or energy to spend on her.

"People don't know how to talk to each other anymore. We're all in our own little bubbles. It used to be common politeness to chitchat about the weather if you were standing in line with someone, or on an elevator or something."

"It's true," she said. "Now it feels like you're invading somebody's personal space if you try to strike up a conversation."

He nodded. "We've lost something—or we're in the process of losing it, anyway. This inability to have a simple back-and-forth about nothing too important is actually damaging the fabric of our society. I, for one, am determined to fight against this tsunami of self-inflicted social isolation." He leaned back in his chair and grinned at her before taking a swig of coffee. "Will you join me, Pinkie?"

She laughed. "You've given this a lot of thought. I bet you work in tech."

He stared at her in surprise. "You are correct. How did you guess that?"

She grinned, pleased with herself. "Well, I always like to guess what people might do and sometimes I get it right. I figured that if you worked in an area related to this topic you feel so passionate about, then you'd probably be a social scientist or something. So, I almost guessed that. But then, I thought you were more likely to be the kind of person to be interested in topics quite different from your work. What kind of tech?"

"Software development. And you?"

"Right now, I'm a paralegal." She couldn't keep the distaste from her voice.

"You don't love it?"

She shook her head, biting into her half-moon cookie. Twenty-eight years old and she had yet to figure out what she wanted to do with her life. She'd wanted to get a master's in education and teach, but Kenny had said they couldn't afford for her to take out even more student loans.

"Your ex-husband lives in Utica?"

She nodded. "That's where we both grew up. Where are you coming from?"

"Just now? Buffalo. Consulting gig."

"Wouldn't it be quicker to fly?"

"Considerably, especially this trip. But I love the train. I take it every opportunity I have. This route down the river is particularly beautiful."

She smiled. "So do I. Love the train."

They stared at each other for a full moment. She lowered her eyes. He cleared his throat.

"So, does that mean you're new to Richmond?" He broke his muffin into quarters and popped one into his mouth.

"Yes."

"How do you like it?"

"I think if I live there another thirty years, I'll still feel like I'm new to Richmond. People are perfectly friendly in that Southern kind of way, but it only goes so far... I haven't found my niche yet."

"Why Richmond?"

"Because that's where I got a job. I figured I had to start over somewhere. It didn't matter too much where."

"Well, do you know anyone in Richmond?"

"I know a few people now, but nobody well."

He studied her.

"What?" she asked nervously.

"That's courageous of you. Starting over somewhere completely new."

She shrugged. "I was running away. I'm not sure that counts as courageous."

They finished their food and coffee in silence, each thinking. Then he stood. "We'd better head back. You go ahead. I need to pick up a couple things."

"Oh," she said, surprised. She shook her head at herself as she headed back to the train. She could not be disappointed he wasn't walking her to her seat, for goodness' sake. He seemed so sweet and attentive, but he probably behaved exactly the same way with everyone. Maybe, in fact, his attentiveness to her was nothing more than him being a Southern gentleman.

When they were both settled into their seats, she said, "I'm going to try to get some more sleep while it's still dark."

"Good idea," he said. "Maybe I will too."

3

ALONG THE HUDSON

They didn't sleep. A woman in the seat behind them began making phone calls to family and friends. Each call began, "I'm so sorry. Did I wake you? I'm still on this train and I'm so bored. This has been the longest ride ever. What are you doing?" After the woman began the fourth call, Rebecca felt ready to jump out of her skin, and her seatmate was laughing with amusement at her consternation.

"Does she think everyone on this train wants to listen to her stupid conversations?" Rebecca hissed. "What is so funny about this? It's so rude. Don't you think it's rude? Or do you think it's okay because she's repairing the 'fabric of society' with all her damn small talk?"

He nodded, laughing, and said, "Touché!"

"I wouldn't care if she was talking to someone in the seat next to her, but hearing half a conversation is so annoying, especially when it sounds like a recording playing the same thing over and over. I just think it's beyond inconsiderate to inflict this on fellow passengers." She flung herself back against her seat. "Thank God there's a quiet car once we leave Penn Station."

"Ah. Are you a quiet car person?"

"Yes. Are you?"

"I will be, unless you object to my company."

"Of course not." She smiled, feeling warm inside.

He turned to her confidingly. "I once rode a train with a divorce lawyer who revealed masses of confidential information about his client to his captive audience. Enough for me to actually figure out who his client was, with a little help from Google."

"That's horrible!" she whispered.

"Yeah, it was pretty bad," he whispered back. "I emailed the woman and advised her to get herself a new attorney."

She stared at him. "Did you really?"

"It would have felt irresponsible not to. What?"

"Nothing, nothing. Just, you're an honest-to-goodness good Samaritan, that's all. Did she fire him?"

"Well, not too long after I sent my email, he did suddenly get very quiet." He laughed softly, gazing at her. "Did anyone ever tell you that you have an enchanting smile?"

She clapped both her hands over her mouth, her cheeks heating up with pleasure.

"Well, that does it," he whispered, still holding her gaze. "I'm not going to say a word about your eyes. Or that dimple."

She lowered her hands. "Stop," she whispered, her heart pounding. "Please, stop." He was flirting with her. He was actually flirting. She didn't know how to do this. She wasn't ready to do this. She looked out the window. "Oh, the river." Dawn turned the sky from black to gray and the Hudson flowed beside them in chilly majesty. "I never remember which side to sit on if I want to see the river."

"I'll give you a trick. People tend to be more politically liberal, or left-leaning, in their youth, the years going uphill, or north. So, if you're going north and you want to sit on the river side, sit on the left. But once people are over the hill and older and wiser, they're more conservative and right-leaning. So, if you're going south, and you want to sit on the river side, sit on the right. Left going north, right going south. That's how I remember. I always want a seat on the river side."

"That's baloney," she said irritably.

"Perhaps, but as a mnemonic device, it works."

"My grandparents are in their eighties, and they would rather write in Mickey Mouse than ever vote for a Republican."

"A shining example of open-minded liberalism if I ever heard one."

She turned to him with sudden urgency. "Please don't tell me you're a Republican."

He laughed, somewhat astonished, but his brown eyes danced. "Treacherous waters here, Pinkie. Are we really going to talk politics? I'm game if you are."

"Please, just tell me. It's not that I can't be friends with someone who's Republican. We can still be friends. I'll just need to work so much harder. Do you know one of the hardest things for me in college was realizing how many Republicans are actually intelligent people? It simply doesn't compute. How do you vote?"

He stopped smiling and studied her for a long moment. "Did you know many parents would rather their child marry someone of a different race or religion than a different political party?"

"You're stalling."

"I'm troubled by how divisive our society has become. That something like this should matter so much."

"I said we could still be friends."

"Do you mean it?" he asked. "Would you really be willing to work so much harder, if it turns out that you don't like the way I vote?"

She stared at him, suddenly afraid that she was wildly out of line. She had friends she'd known for years that she had never had this conversation with. Why was it so important to have it with him, this stranger? Why did it feel safe enough to have it with him?

"Yes," she said. "I would."

He nodded. "All right, then. So, I do this very unusual thing of actually listening to what all the candidates have to say about a whole variety of issues, and I observe their character and temperament as well, and I make sure to never enter the polling site without being able to make a truly informed decision based on the candidates themselves, regardless of party..." He stopped talking and grinned devilishly at her. "My goodness, Pinkie, you are literally squirming with anxiety. I am a registered Independent."

She relaxed against the seat and exhaled. "Okay. That I can live with."

"However," he added, "I am related to many people who would prefer to write in a Disney character than ever vote for a Democrat. I think the preference is for Goofy, not Mickey Mouse. But if I were a registered Republican...?"

She turned to him, smiling. "We could still be friends. I meant it. I'm Rebecca."

"Craig." He extended his hand, and she shook it. "Nice to meet you, Rebecca. I'm afraid I'm still going to call you Pinkie."

"I'm sorry, did I wake you?" the woman behind them said into her phone.

Rebecca banged the back of her head against the seat with a groan and looked at Craig miserably. "I didn't notice when she stopped talking enough to appreciate her being quiet!" she whispered.

"I just asked if I woke you up," the woman said, raising her voice. "Do you have your hearing aids in? This has been the longest train ride ever and I am so bored."

"Oh, my God!" Rebecca whispered. "I am seriously going to lose my mind. I'm sorry. I know my inner toddler is showing, but I can't help it. I can't stand it when people are so inconsiderate. I wish I could get up the nerve to say something to her."

Craig held a hand over his mouth to silence his laughter. "I wouldn't take her on. Choose your battles. I have a better idea. Café car? You don't happen to play Spit, do you?"

"I am a champion Spit player. You don't have cards, do you?"

"I don't go anywhere—especially on a long train trip— without cards." He pulled a well-worn pack out of his jacket pocket.

She led the way. In one of the connections between cars, she slipped on the wet floor and almost fell, but he caught her and steadied her. She could feel the sturdiness of his chest at her back, his hands on her arms.

"You all right now?" he said softly in her ear.

She nodded, and he let go.

4

PENN STATION

After one round, they acknowledged that Rebecca's mummified finger put her at too great a disadvantage for Spit, and they switched to Gin Rummy, which they played for the next three hours. During their five-hour layover at Penn Station, they walked about. He insisted on carrying her heavy suitcase in one hand, in addition to his duffle bag and backpack, until she proved herself even more stubborn by refusing to walk one more step unless he gave her something to carry.

"Please don't ever tell my mother I let you do this," he said, sliding his backpack over her shoulders.

An older woman stepped in front of them, a wide smile on her face. "I'm sorry to interrupt you," she said. "I just have to say, I've been watching you, and you just look like the cutest couple."

Rebecca blushed. "We—we're not a couple," she stammered. "We're just... friends?" She looked at Craig for confirmation. He raised an eyebrow at her, a slight smile on his face.

"Thank you," he said to the woman. "Have a nice day."

They told stories of their families, their college experiences, their relationships. He had had a couple of serious girlfriends, and confessed he'd spent the last couple of years recovering from a broken heart.

"It turned out I wasn't ambitious enough for her."

"You? I would imagine you have to be fairly ambitious to be in software development. I say this knowing nothing about computers, but seriously? Don't you make a decent salary?"

"Yes, but she didn't want to have to work, and she wanted a McMansion and membership at a fancy country club, and my salary would not accommodate that lifestyle."

Rebecca shook her head. "You could not pay me enough to live in a McMansion. Sorry. I'm not meaning to criticize your ex, but don't you think that's ostentatious? Like, you just want to let people know you have money?"

He gazed at her thoughtfully and nodded. "That is, actually, what I think. So, you don't like being a paralegal. If money were no object and you had nothing holding you back and you could do anything in the world, what would you do?"

"I can't imagine a world in which money is no object and nothing held me back."

"Try."

She smiled. "I love children. I would be an elementary school teacher. My ex-husband did not approve. *Those who can't do, teach,* you know."

"That is an expression that only truly stupid people say."

"You're talking about my ex-husband."

"Apparently, I am. Teaching is the most noble profession. I believe that. Teachers change people's lives."

"Well, anyway. I have a lot more debt still from college to tackle before I can even think about getting a master's in education."

"It sounds like you've had your dreams squashed a bit."

"Yes." She told him about Kenny, how hard she'd fallen for

his boyish charm, and how devastating it had been to discover how completely she had misread his character.

"It was my fault," she said. "I was foolish to jump into marriage with him when I really didn't know him very long. I acted more out of fear than love. My parents moved away, and I didn't have anywhere to live. We were dating, and he asked me to move in with him and his mom, and she didn't want us living there together if we weren't married. So, we got married. It was all just till we could get our feet on the ground, I thought. And I think she thought being married might make him grow up. After a while, it became clear to me that he didn't consider our living arrangement temporary. And then, he started to get pretty controlling and demanding. And not once in our entire marriage did he ever do the dishes!"

Craig stopped walking and ran a gentle finger around the rim of her ear. "You've got steam coming out," he said, looking puzzled. He glanced at her other ear. "Out of both of them."

For a moment, she stared at him with confusion. Then she burst out laughing and pushed her hand against his chest. "I'm sorry," she said. "I know I still have a lot of resentment, but I am going to get over it. I'm tired of feeling so angry. But it was my fault. Like I said, I hadn't known him very long before I married him."

"It sounds like you were foolish to marry him," Craig said. "But I don't think the length of time you know someone should be the determining factor. I think sometimes people just know when they meet the right person. Especially when they've had time to figure out what they don't want."

She smiled. "Have you figured out what you don't want, Craig?"

He returned her smile with an expression of utter solemnity. "I have, Pinkie. Have you?"

They stared at each other for a long, quiet moment.

"I know I don't want anything serious," she said. "At least not now."

"Don't worry. I'm not proposing," he said. "But I would like to hold your hand—the one not in the cast. Would that be okay?"

She swallowed, staring into his warm brown eyes. Then she held out her right hand, and he clasped it. They strolled through the crowds, hand in hand, in comfortable silence. Too comfortable. She stopped and pulled her hand away.

"What's happening here?" she whispered in alarm.

"Don't fight it, Pinkie." He gazed at her tenderly. "Please. I have a feeling."

She turned away. "You don't understand. I just left my ex-husband. Hours ago. Well, maybe hours and hours ago, but still hours."

"I do understand. You just told me all about it."

"I can't do this." She brought her good hand up to her temple and pressed. "I must be out of my mind. What am I thinking?" She turned back to him. He had on that stubborn face she'd glimpsed a couple of times now, but this time it didn't flit away. "I'm sorry. It's not you. You are obviously a wonderful, gorgeous, amazing man and I would be beyond lucky to ever have a man like you interested in me. But now is not the time for me to begin something with someone. If that's what you're thinking. Is that what you're thinking?"

"We've already begun something, Pinkie."

"But I can't." Her heart pounded in panic. "I simply can't. I'm sorry."

"Listen. How about you just give me your phone number and let me call you and take you out on a date?"

She shook her head.

"Think about it," he said. "Just think about it."

5

ASHLAND

They sat in the Penn Station passenger lounge, beside each other, in silence. They boarded the train to Virginia and sat in the quiet car together. He made no attempt to converse with her, but took out his e-reader and seemed focused on that. She wanted to ask what he was reading. She wanted to know more about his family. She wanted to know what kinds of activities he enjoyed, besides card games, which he was better at than she was, she had discovered, to her astonishment. She wanted to get to know him.

She wanted to give him her phone number.

But every time she began to say that, panic overwhelmed her. She needed time to be by herself, to figure out who she was. She simply could not jump into another relationship, mere hours after leaving her ex-husband for good. Who ever heard of something so stupid? It wouldn't be fair to Craig. That would make him a rebound relationship. She liked him too much to do that to him.

The train stopped in Philadelphia. "I could be wrong, but I actually think you want to give me your phone number," Craig whispered. "Is it possible I'm right?"

"It's possible," she whispered back. Then she shook her head miserably. She had to be strong. "I don't want you to be a rebound relationship. It's not fair to you."

"Pinkie," he said, looking at her sternly. "You know that's not what this is as well as I do. Stop fighting it. Sometimes serendipitous things just happen this way."

"No, they don't. Not to me, anyway. And I don't want to be hurt again and I don't want to hurt you."

The train stopped in Baltimore. "Listen. I really like you," Craig said. "I mean, I really like you. And honestly, your relationship didn't end yesterday. It ended months ago. And I am not asking you to move in with me or marry me. Seriously. I'd like to go out with you. We can take this as slow as you want."

"I'm sorry," she said stubbornly. "I wish I could, but I'm too afraid. I'm not ready."

The conductor stood at their seats. "This is the quiet car," he said. "If you want to speak, there are other cars."

Craig gestured his willingness to move, but she shook her head. He settled into his chair, resigned. As they approached his stop, he took out a crumpled brown paper bag from his backpack, wrote his name and phone number on it, and handed it to her.

"Okay," he said. "Here's my number. I hope you call."

She took the bag and held it in her lap, her hands trembling.

"Now arriving in Ashland, Virginia, the center of the universe," the conductor cried.

Rebecca smiled. "Does he always say that?"

"Often," Craig said, smiling back at her sadly. "It's an Ashland thing." He stood, reached for her suitcase on the overhead rack, and carried it to the front of the car. That was so considerate of him. It would have been very hard for her to get it down on her own. He was truly a gentleman. She would remember this day for the rest of her life. She knew she would.

The train pulled into the station. He stood, looking down the aisle at her with frustration. Still clutching the paper bag in her hands, she left her seat and walked toward him, not knowing what to say, but knowing that she needed to say something.

"Ready to give me your phone number?" he asked.

"Please forgive me," she said. She reached up and kissed him on the lips. "Goodbye, Craig. Thank you. For what it's worth, this has probably been the happiest day of my life."

He gazed at her solemnly. "Okay. 'Bye, Pinkie."

"Are you getting off, Sir?" the conductor asked.

"I am," Craig said. He shouldered his duffle bag and backpack, glanced at her one more time, and walked down the steps and off the train. "Careful," he called up to her, gesturing to the bag. "Don't crumple that too much."

She waved and walked back to her seat and looked for him out the window. He had turned his back and was walking away. She glanced down at the crumpled bag in her hands. She'd better not lose his number. She glanced out the window again at his retreating figure. She opened the bag and found two slightly squashed half-moon cookies. A lump formed in her throat. Tears watered her eyes. She never thought she'd have one of these in Virginia. He was so sweet to think of this.

She jumped up, grabbing her coat and purse, and ran to the front of the car. "Wait!" she told the conductor who had already pulled up the stairs. "I'm getting off here!"

The man looked at her like she was crazy. "You're going to Richmond, Ma'am."

"I'm getting off here. Please. Please let me off."

Reluctantly, he lowered the stairs again. Rebecca ran down them. Craig was heading down the main street toward a parking area. She ran after him.

"Craig!" she called out.

He stopped walking and stood for a moment, still facing away. She ran toward him.

He turned around and looked at her gravely, not smiling. "You had me worried there, Pinkie." He'd actually been upset. She could see it in his face.

"You gave me half-moon cookies."

He breathed a sigh of relief. "Thank God I followed my intuition on that."

"Where did you get them?"

"Albany."

"Albany!" Her eyes flooded with tears. "I'm sorry," she said, knocking her pinkie cast against her glasses as she wiped her face. "No one's ever done anything so sweet for me before."

"Pinkie," Craig said. "Where's your suitcase?"

Behind her came the rumbling sounds of the train leaving the station.

"Oh, no!" she said, looking after the departing train.

"Come on." He unlocked his car with an automatic key. "We can beat the train to Richmond. Maybe. You better call though and make sure they leave your suitcase there."

She ran around to the passenger seat and slid in.

He started the car, unsuccessfully trying to repress a grin.

"What are you thinking?" she asked.

He shrugged. "I'm thinking how much fun I'm going to have telling our children and grandchildren that you were chasing after me from the first day I met you."

"You really didn't give me a choice."

"Oh, yes, I did. I was very tempted to take your suitcase, so you'd have to chase after me, but I restrained myself. No, you definitely chased after me of your own volition."

"Craig!" she cried. "You can't tell everybody that."

"You kissed me first, too. Don't even try to twist your tale on that one." He laughed at her dismay.

She bit her lip, then laughed too. "Oh goodness. I don't even know how I'm going to get home now."

"Yes, you do," he said. "First, we're going to pick up your suitcase, and then I'm going to drive you home. I may even walk you to your door."

She opened the crinkled paper bag, pulled out a mushed-up half-moon cookie, and took a bite. It tasted better than she ever remembered.

FORMER
THINGS

A Short Story

FORMER THINGS

The public viewing was over. Now it was just him. In the quiet hallway outside the sanctuary of the First Baptist Church of Haverly, Virginia, Sean Timmerman stood before his grandmother's casket, looking at her still features for the final time. He tried to imprint them on his memory: her short, fine hair, bright red, because that was his grandmother. No dignified gray for her. Nose with a slight bump at the top. Large mouth with her favorite pink lipstick, pressed into a semblance of a smile. Pale blue dress with brass buttons running down the middle. Hands folded one over the other... missing something.

Oh, right. Her diamond ring, which the funeral home director had just reminded him to take off before they closed the casket. It was in his pocket now. He had no idea what he was supposed to do with it. Gran had told him to sell it, if he couldn't find a use for it, but insisted he not bury her with it.

Once she stopped fighting the fact that she was dying, they'd set up a hospital bed in her bedroom.

"All the important papers are in that bottom drawer," she'd said, pointing to her bureau. "Don't bother with them till after I die. I hate to leave you, Sean. Is there anyone...?"

He shook his head. She'd turned her head away, brow crinkled, as if in pain.

"Something hurting you, Gran?"

"I'm sorry. Maybe I should have told you..."

"Told me what, Gran?"

He waited for her to finish that sentence, but she just squeezed her eyes shut.

That was the last coherent conversation he'd had with her. Her pain got worse. The doctor increased her morphine. Dying was harder than it looked. Took longer than he expected, too. Five nights of sleeping in a recliner by her hospital bed, waking up every time her breathing changed. And then she'd slipped off when he'd taken a bathroom break. Didn't want to die in front of him, he guessed. She was always trying to spare him pain. He wished she'd been able to spare herself some, too.

Special dates always stuck in his mind. June 16, 1983, would be one of those dates: the day his grandmother died. To add to November 2, 1973, the day his mother had died of cancer and a broken heart. There was no particular date on which his father had morphed from distant to cheating husband, deadbeat to absent dad, self-centered to negligent son.

The sound of a throat clearing jolted Sean out of his reverie. Pastor Gentry, wearing a long black robe and white stole, emerged from his office down the hall and walked toward Sean. He'd come to visit Gran several times at home. Nice man. When he reached the casket, he stood beside Sean, head bowed. Then he snorted and clapped a hand to his mouth.

Sean glanced at him, unsettled.

"Sorry." The pastor tried to wipe the smile off his face. "She just... she just insisted that red was her natural color. With a straight face. Just daring me to doubt her."

Sean nodded, pressing his lips together. Then he snorted too, and a laugh rose from his belly. He pressed a hand to his forehead. "Sorry, Gran," he said. "I'm trying to be serious here, but with your pastor cracking jokes, it's hard."

Pastor Gentry composed himself. "Do you think your father's going to make it?"

"Why would he make this?" Sean said bitterly. "He missed everything else in her life."

His aimless father had drifted out of their lives on a quaalude high. Missed Sean's mom's funeral, Sean's high school graduation. Left Sean to function as both grandson and son to Gran. Like now. Taking care of funeral arrangements. Though he was glad to do it. She'd been there for him when no one else had.

"It's his loss, Sean. You were everything to her and you're here. The church has filled up. You ready?"

Sean bent over, pressed one last kiss on his grandmother's cold forehead, and then turned away. He looked at his hands. There was still green paint around his nails that he hadn't been able to scrape off from the last house he'd been painting just a couple of weeks ago.

He followed Gran's closed casket into the sanctuary. Pastor Gentry gestured to the front pew. Sean looked around before he sat. He was the youngest person here by decades. There were more people than he expected. Maybe forty. He recognized a few of them, mostly Gran's church friends.

Catherine Henry was there, looking regal, perfectly coiffed hair, posture like a queen. Sarah's grandmother. And his own grandmother's nemesis. She'd visited Gran a couple of times. Brought one of those prayer shawls that their craft group used to knit together. Then picked up some old argument they had. He'd made the mistake of leaving them alone. Had to rush back in when he heard their raised voices and ask her to leave. Who picks a fight with a dying woman? The only thing those two women ever agreed on was that each thought her own grandchild was too good for the other's grandchild.

Honestly, he was surprised Mrs. Henry had come. Probably wanted gloating rights for having lived longer. Everything was a competition between them. How many conversations had Gran started by saying, "You wouldn't believe what Catherine the Great said at craft group today! That woman thinks her shit don't stink. And she calls *me* vulgar."

With no warning, another snort erupted from his nose. He whipped around, plopped down on the pew, and dropped his face in his hands. Better that people here think he was crying than laughing. When he could raise his head with a solemn face, he looked at the pastor, who winked at him and then stood, recited some scripture, and invited them all to stand for the opening hymn, "Amazing Grace."

Sean pulled a hymnal from the shelf beneath his pew, stood, and glanced behind him one more time.

There was Sarah, standing at the front door, waiting for an usher to hand her a program.

He hadn't seen her in three years, but she was unmistakably the woman who had broken his heart all those summers ago. Her wavy auburn hair was longer now and hung loose about her pale face. Navy-blue suit hugging her curves, eyes on the carpet. She looked sad. Nervous.

Lovely.

What was she doing here? She'd made absolutely no contact and now she thought she'd just drop in on his grandmother's funeral? She barely knew his grandmother. Well, he guessed that wasn't exactly true. Sarah had come over for Sunday brunch a few times that summer. She and Gran had gotten along great. But Gran never forgave her for hurting him, for saying she didn't want to settle for a housepainter, that he should be more ambitious.

He was plenty ambitious. He'd aimed to be a top-notch housepainter. Now he was one, with his own company to boot, people working for him.

He stared at her until other people followed his lead, glancing back at her, too. He faced forward again and flipped open his hymnal, but couldn't sing. His throat constricted.

What was she doing here? Was there any chance she...? He closed his eyes. *Don't hope,* he warned himself. *Don't hope.*

The pastor motioned them all to sit down, welcomed them, said some funny things about Gran that made everyone laugh, led them in prayer, and then read the Twenty-third Psalm.

The Lord is my shepherd, I shall not want. He maketh me to lie down in green pastures...

Sean glanced back again. Now Sarah was sitting on the aisle seat beside her grandmother, looking straight ahead. She seemed to feel his eyes on her. The muscles in her face tightened. Was she going to ignore him? She raised her chin slightly, jaw clenched, and looked at him, holding his gaze. Maybe she nodded. It was such a slight gesture; he wasn't sure. He could hardly breathe. He couldn't believe she was here. Her lips opened, and she mouthed, "Hi." Smile so sweet, just like he remembered.

He smiled back. He couldn't stop himself. Then he forced himself to turn away, face forward. *Don't hope, Sean.*

How did she even know about Gran's funeral? Mrs. Henry wouldn't have encouraged her to come. Would she? To say that Sarah's grandmother hadn't been a fan of their relationship was putting it mildly. She'd been convinced Sean would turn out to be a replica of his father, to whom he bore such a strong physical resemblance. Just assumed he'd also move from job to job and woman to woman, unlike the stuffy, high-powered lawyer her own son had become. That's what Sarah's grandmother and father wanted for her. What Sarah had decided she wanted, too.

Last he heard, she'd met some lawyer, was close to being engaged.

"Sean," Pastor Gentry said, in a tone that made it clear he had called his name before.

Sean stood, clenched his hands and released them, and walked to the lectern. He didn't know what he said. He'd thought of a few stories to tell, and he guessed he told them because people were laughing. He tried to avoid Sarah's face while he spoke, but he glanced at her once and she was laughing, too. And crying. Wiping her fingers across her cheeks. As if Gran had meant something to her. Mrs. Henry was also crying. He had no idea what to make of that.

Finally, he thanked them all for being there and sat down again.

The pastor talked some about heaven and God wiping away all the tears from their eyes. About no more death or sorrow or crying or pain, about former things passing away.

Sean wished some former things had never passed away.

It occurred to him he wasn't the youngest one here anymore. Sarah was two years younger. Twenty-four, that would be. Her birthday was last month. May 7, 1959. He'd seen her for the first time on July 4, three years ago. The details of those two summer months were etched on his memory.

She'd been wearing a bright red, spaghetti strap dress at dinner with a group of snooty girls at the Haverly Country Club. He'd waited on her table. They'd noticed the paint staining his hands from his work painting houses earlier that day, before he started the evening shift at the club. Her friends had made obnoxious remarks about their waiter not having clean hands, though he'd scrubbed his hands raw and still couldn't get the paint off. She'd come back to the kitchen to apologize for their behavior.

Then she waited around until his shift ended. They took a

walk on the golf course under a full moon. First side by side. Then holding hands and talking. Found they had so much in common. Both had lost their mothers when they were teenagers. Both were close to their grandmothers and staying with them for the summer. Both had already seen *The Empire Strikes Back* four times. She said he looked like Harrison Ford. He didn't think so, but he was flattered. They were surprised they hadn't met before, but then again, he and Gran weren't in the country club crowd, and he'd never worked there before, so it wasn't so surprising, really.

When they got to the seventeenth hole, they stopped talking. At the eighteenth hole, they stopped walking.

By morning, he was in love.

Pastor Gentry cleared his throat. Sean shook himself. As the organ played, he stood and walked beside the pastor down the center aisle behind Gran's casket. They reached Sarah's pew. The procession paused. One of the bier's front wheels had snagged on a slight ridge in the carpet. He had to stand right there, inches from her. For a moment, he faced forward, thinking, *Come on, God. Really? Is this amusing to you?*

Then he glanced at her. She was looking at him tenderly, her light brown eyes watering. Those sweet freckles still dusting her cheeks. Those full lips, half-smiling.

And then her hand clasped his. And, oh, God, it was like an electric shock, a jolt of energy through his whole body, making him long for things he thought he'd given up longing for. He closed his eyes. Squeezed her fingers. Didn't want to let go— wasn't sure he even could. He never thought he'd hold her hand again. Her hand with no ring. She wasn't engaged.

But they were moving again. The pastor nudged him. He let her fingers slide away and followed the casket out of the church. The June day was warm, sunny, cheery. He put a hand over his eyes to block the glare. Watched the pallbearers lift the casket off the bier, load it into the hearse, shut the door. Then he got in his car and followed the hearse to the cemetery. Soon, Gran's casket lay on planks above an open pit.

He wondered who would come to this part, the burial. Wondered if she would come.

Don't hope, Sean.

But there she was, her arm linked through her grandmother's, walking slowly in his direction.

Pastor Gentry spoke a few more words, prayed again, nodded to Sean that it was over. Sean felt a pang of guilt at being more focused on Sarah than his grandmother. He laid a hand on her casket. *'Bye, Gran. Love you.*

Then he looked around for Sarah. She stood with her back toward him, talking with some of her grandmother's friends. She'd taken off her jacket, revealing a sleeveless white top, her delectable shoulders and arms covered with light freckles. Suddenly, he smelled coconut and strawberries. Like the suntan lotion he used to rub onto those shoulders. And the scent of her shampoo when he kissed her ears. She used to love that.

"Sean?" Pastor Gentry said.

"Sorry. Could you repeat that?"

"I said I understand people have been dropping off quite a bit of food at your grandmother's house."

Sean nodded. "Yep. Not sure how much they think one guy can eat."

Pastor Gentry smiled. "Perhaps you want to invite everyone over to help you eat it."

Sean gave a short laugh. "Oh. That's what it's for? Sure. The place is a bit of a mess, though."

"I believe members of the craft group are getting everything sorted out. I wouldn't worry."

The pastor made a general announcement, and everyone headed back to their cars. Sean sat in the driver's seat, waiting for Sarah and Mrs. Henry to walk past his car. When they did, he rolled down his window.

"Sarah?" First time he'd spoken her name aloud in three years.

She turned, her arm linked through her grandmother's. Her grandmother was patting her hand, as if Sarah needed some kind of reassurance. "Yes?"

"You coming over to the house?" He tried not to look too hopeful, but he did smile, silently urging her to say yes.

She smiled back. "Yes."

His heart thudded. "See you there."

"Yes," she said again.

He waited till they moved farther down the road, then started his car and headed out of the cemetery, leading a procession of cars past horse farms and rolling green hills to his grandmother's house in the woods. Inside, the place looked resplendent, with casserole dishes and ham biscuits and multihued gelatin salads spread out all over the dining room table. Bottles of soda and pitchers of iced tea and lemonade lined one kitchen counter. Brownies, cakes, and pies filled another. His stomach growled. He couldn't remember the last time he'd eaten. The smells and colorful culinary displays were making him hungry.

One of his grandmother's craft group friends handed him a plate overflowing with food and a large glass of iced tea. He took a sip and almost choked, it was so sweet. He was used to Gran's unsweetened tea.

His grandmother's house—well, his house now—filled with people who made themselves at home in the kitchen, living room, dining room, and on the porch, too. Conversation buzzed, quiet at first, then getting noisier. People laughing. Telling Gran stories.

He stood on the front porch, waiting for Sarah. Here they

came, walking down the long driveway. He felt bad they had to park so far away. Mrs. Henry looked like she was having trouble keeping her balance, but she still held that erect posture that used to annoy Gran so much. *Thinks she's queen of the craft group.* Sean smiled. Gran thought *she* was queen of the craft group.

"Sean," one of his grandmother's friends said. "Sit. Eat something." The woman took the glass from his hand, set it on a table, pushed him down onto a wicker loveseat, and handed him a fork wrapped in a paper napkin.

"Yes, Ma'am," Sean said, embarrassed to be sitting down the moment that Sarah walked up the porch steps.

Her grandmother released her arm and followed the other woman inside, leaving him and Sarah alone on the porch. To his surprise, Sarah sat down beside him. The loveseat was small enough to make this a tight squeeze. The whole left side of his body pressed against hers. She didn't try to inch away. Neither did he.

"Hi." She kept her voice low. "Is this okay? For me to sit here?"

He nodded. "I didn't expect you." He kept his voice low, too.

"Oh." She lowered her eyes. "I thought maybe you did."

"Why would I?"

Her brow crinkled. "I can leave if you want." She made an attempt to rise.

"No!" He jerked, almost losing control of his plate. She caught one side of it and balanced it on both their knees. "I don't want you to leave. I'm glad you're here." When she didn't say anything, he added, "Hungry? Help me out?"

"Happy to." She took a ham biscuit off his plate. "Apparently, your grandmother told my grandmother she hoped I would come."

"To her funeral?" Sean tried not to gape. "Sorry, I almost don't believe that. She wasn't your biggest fan."

"I know. She thought I was hoity-toity. She told me so. She thought you could do better." Sarah paused, then continued, "My grandmother is impressed by how well you took care of your grandmother when she got sick. She said she was wrong about you."

Sean was so shocked to hear this, he couldn't think how to respond.

After a moment of heavy silence, Sarah said, "Is there someone special in your life?"

He could see her light freckles up close now, her full lips, her gentle brown eyes with mascara smeared underneath, from crying. Felt the warmth of her thigh pressing against his. "Maybe." He held her gaze. "You?"

She didn't take her eyes off his. "I don't know." She swallowed, looking down. "You're still painting houses?"

He saw her noticing the paint remnants on his hands. "Yeah. Still hard to get the paint off."

She smiled, as if she were also remembering the night they met. "Do you still like it?"

He nodded again. "Love it. Got more work than I can handle."

"That's great. Where?"

"About an hour from here. What about you? How'd you like law school?"

"I didn't love it. I finished, and I've got a job, but..."

"Did you fall in love with New York like you thought you would?"

She seemed surprised, as if she expected him to know the answer to this, then turned away, shrugging. "Not really."

After a moment, he handed her his glass. "Thirsty? It's sweet."

She took a sip and almost choked. "Very sweet." She stood

up, cradling her elbows. "I wasn't sure you would even talk to me. Or want me to be here."

He put down the plate and stood, too. "Why?"

She shrugged. "Your grandmother told me you'd moved on."

He stared at her. "When did she tell you that?"

She looked confused. "When I visited her, to give her the letters. I came twice. Since I didn't have your address." Her voice trembled. "Did you even bother to read them?"

The porch door opened. Mrs. Henry came out and handed Sarah a plate of food.

"Grandma, can we please have some privacy?" Sarah said.

At the same time Sean said, "Sarah. What letters?"

Mrs. Henry glared at Sean and shook her head. "She didn't give them to you, did she? I asked her again the last time I saw her if she just threw them away, and she said 'of course not' but she wouldn't confirm that she gave them to you. Did she even tell you Sarah visited her?"

Sean stared at her, a sour taste rising to his mouth.

"Why wouldn't she?" Sarah pressed a hand to her heart, looking horrified. "I didn't think she hated me."

Sean closed his eyes. He'd told Gran not to talk to him about Sarah. Ever. It was too painful. But he didn't know Sarah had tried to reach out to him. Had visited Gran. Had written to him. Surely, Gran would have realized he'd want to know that.

"She didn't hate you, dear, or she wouldn't have specifically asked me to invite you to come to her funeral," Mrs. Henry said. "She loved Sean, and she probably was afraid of you hurting him again. I think she was also a selfish woman who didn't want to share him either, at least not while she was alive. Sorry to speak ill of the dead, Sean, but that's just my personal opinion."

Sean was too bewildered to feel anything more than passing irritation at Sarah's grandmother's "personal opinion."

"She said she didn't throw them away, Sean," Mrs. Henry repeated.

All the important papers are in that bottom drawer, Gran had said.

Without answering, Sean went inside, weaving his way through the crowd till he reached his grandmother's room, knelt by her bureau, and opened the bottom drawer. On top of a stack of papers labeled "Important Documents" were two sealed envelopes with his name in Sarah's handwriting. He stood and looked at Sarah, who had followed him into the room. Her mouth hung open, her eyes wide with hurt.

"I can't believe this," he whispered.

"Why would she...?"

"I told her not to talk to me about you. But I didn't know..."

Turning away from her, he looked out the window at the thick woods and thrust his hands in his pockets. His fingers jammed against something sharp. He pulled out his hand, holding his grandmother's diamond ring, which he stared at, as if he'd never seen it before. He looked at Sarah, whose eyes flashed wide at the sight of the ring.

"She told me to sell it if I couldn't find a use for it," Sean said.

"Sell it! You're not going to sell it, are you?"

He studied the ring. "No." He slid it back in his pocket.

She exhaled in relief. "Good."

He looked up and held her gaze. "I think I'd rather find a use for it." He knew there was a question in his eyes.

Her gaze grew shy. She turned to look out the window. They stood side by side, quiet, hearing the gentle murmur of voices from the front of the house.

"Sarah?"

"Yes?"

"What did they say? The letters?"

In a husky voice, she said, "That I was sorry. That I loved

you. That I thought we could work things out. That I hoped it wasn't too late."

He nodded. "I would have read them. I would have written back."

"Really?"

He nodded again, then turned to face her. "Is it too late?"

She looked up at him, her eyes shining. A tear trickled down. He brushed his thumb across her cheek. Former things, passing away. Her arms encircled his waist. She buried her face in his neck and shook her head. Wrapping his arms around her, he pulled her close, kissing her temple. He smelled strawberries.

"God, I've missed you, Sarah."

IT'S UP TO YOU,

New York

A Short Story

A RIDE ON THE A TRAIN

A hoarse cry rang through the subway car, making Jean Dennin flinch and dart a glance over her shoulder. A woman who looked to be the same age as herself, which is to say, middle-aged, had slumped from her seat to the subway floor. Unlike herself, the woman wore no pants. Her pale, exposed legs and feet splayed at awkward angles.

Oh God.

Jean faced forward again.

"Help me, help me!" the woman cried. "I can't get up. Will someone please help me?"

Jean looked out the window, seeing nothing in the dark but her own reflection. She seemed to be forgetting how to breathe. What was a decent human being supposed to do in a situation like this? The woman on the floor was obviously troubled. Jean had only been in New York City for two weeks, but that was long enough for her to know that no woman found herself on the A train without pants on, not to mention all those bags on the seats next to her, without being troubled in some major way.

Around Jean, other passengers sat motionless. Jean glanced back again, furtively. The woman reached for a black plastic bag that had fallen to the floor beside her, pulled out a Subway sandwich, turkey it looked like, and took a bite. So, she couldn't be badly hurt.

"Please help me!" the woman cried again, her voice garbled because of the food in her mouth, though it still managed to carry through the subway car. "I can't get up."

Oh, God, please help her. Somebody, please help her.

Several seats in front of Jean, a broad-shouldered man wearing an orange vest with yellow stripes identifying him as a Metropolitan Transit Authority worker, roused himself from a slumped position. He looked exhausted. Jean wondered if he had just come off duty. Clasping his hands together momentarily, he stared out the window of the moving train into the dark subway tunnel, then stood and made his way to the distraught woman on the floor. It would take someone as strong as that man to lift her back up to her seat, which he did. As she requested, he covered her naked legs with her coat, handed her the plastic bag containing the rest of her sandwich, and quietly urged her to put her pants back on. Then he returned to his seat, leaned his head into the wall, and closed his eyes. He had a full head of dark brown hair with silver strands sprinkled throughout, and a network of fine wrinkles radiating from his eyelids.

A true good Samaritan. Unlike herself.

Another quick glance behind her confirmed that the woman who had fallen sat calmly on the seat now, coat over her legs, eating her sandwich.

Jean could breathe again and focus on the goal of her trip: visiting her beloved aunt, finally, and through her own means for the first time. From the time she was a teenager through her early forties, Aunt Celia had paid for Jean's trips east, thwarting first her parents' and then Todd's insistence that they couldn't afford for her to abandon her family and flit off to New York for a few days every couple of years.

Jean had paid for this trip east and for her entire relocation to Manhattan. She was proud that she was making positive changes happen for herself, and grateful for the lifelong role model her aunt had been for her. Aunt Celia believed happy things were in store for those who looked for them, that a hopeful spirit and desire to see good in the world would never let you down, and that there was always beauty and love to be found if you were the type of person who refused to stop searching for it. That's who her aunt was. That was the kind of person Jean wanted to be near. The kind of person she wanted to be, too.

In all her previous visits, she'd never been out to Far Rockaway. She still couldn't believe this was her new life, that she no longer lived in Baraboo, Wisconsin, but in the actual Big Apple.

Twelve years ago, on Jean's last visit to her aunt's beloved basement apartment on Manhattan's Lower East Side, where the window view showed pedestrians from the knee down, Aunt Celia had gone out for bagels and not returned. Jean and her cousin Marie had spent three days frantically trying to find her. They finally did, in Bellevue Hospital. When they walked into the hospital room that she shared with three other patients, Aunt Celia greeted them warmly, said she was so enjoying her vacation and just loved her room with a view. Jean and Marie stood at the window, looking out over the majestic East River, knowing there was no way Aunt Celia could safely return home.

Jean returned to Wisconsin to take care of her ailing parents, leaving Marie, who lived just north of the city in White Plains, with the bulk of the decision-making, with the end result of Aunt Celia's relocation to the Sunset Care Nursing Residence in Far Rockaway, the outer edge of Queens, New York. Their aunt had made it clear she never wanted to leave New York City and, technically, Far Rockaway was part of New York City. The train had come above ground now and the magnificent ocean view Jean saw outside her window made that hard to believe.

They'd stayed in touch through calls and cards, though in the last few years, those coming from her aunt had slowed, then stopped. Never had so many years passed between their in-person visits. Part of Jean hoped Aunt Celia's cognitive issues would make her unaware of exactly how long it had been. But guilt was a useless emotion, and what, after all, could she have done differently? Todd's bombshell had dropped the week she returned from that last trip to New York.

Oh, Todd. Halfway through community college, this suave, handsome man had swept her off her feet and out of her parents' home with an enthusiasm for adventure and activity that thrilled her, contrasting as it did with her parents' staid frugality and accompanying disapproval of anything that veered from the dull routine of their lives. Her parents' dislike of Todd hadn't shocked her. Aunt Celia's had. Jean initially attributed her aunt's dislike to not having time to get to know him. During their courtship, Todd seemed delighted with Jean's ideas about leaving Baraboo and moving to a city somewhere, possibly New York.

But the children came quickly, and she learned the hard way that Todd considered childcare entirely her responsibility, as she wasn't bringing in any income. Adventures became his prerogative alone. He didn't want a partner, just an audience, someone to hear about his games, his sports, his trips. There was no room and no budget for the rest of the family to be part of his fun. As soon as the kids were in school, Jean finished her coursework and got herself certified as a medical technician, but working only part time, she remained dependent on her increasingly absent husband.

Still, the other woman and the divorce caught her by surprise, as did the need to become a caregiver for her father and mother, whammed by Parkinson's and breast cancer, respectively. She hadn't set foot outside Wisconsin for years. It had been all she could do to take care of herself and her kids and her parents, never mind holding down a job, keeping the house running, and taking care of Trixie, the 180-pound Saint Bernard that Todd had insisted on adopting and then refused to take with him when he left.

Then Jean's parents died within two months of each other. The kids graduated from college and didn't come home. The dog died, and the house expanded with emptiness and haunting memories, of the kids when they were little and sweet, of Todd when he was still in love with her, of all those times when she thought they were a happy family.

Jean pressed a hand to her pounding heart and forced herself to look out the window at the rolling dark blue waters of the Atlantic and the expansive cerulean sky.

Breathe.

At least she wasn't stuck in that airless, toxic, bereft space anymore. Jean had felt herself slipping into a depression, but she had caught herself, and out of sheer will, soldiered forward, discovering within herself the spirit Aunt Celia recognized in her as a young girl. She sold her parents' house and her own, found herself a job as a medical technician at Columbia Presbyterian Hospital in New York City, rented a sweet little studio apartment in Inwood, the northernmost tip of Manhattan, and moved across the country. While Jean suspected her children thought she had lost her mind, she could also tell they were excited for her. She told herself she was giving them living proof that it was truly never too late to begin a new adventure.

And it wasn't. Was it? She was doing now what she had intended to do thirty years ago, following the dream she had let Todd talk her out of, leaving her small town behind, and making a life for herself in New York City, just like Aunt Celia had done.

What a flurry of color and sparkle her aunt had been when Jean was a child, bursting through the door of their gray Wisconsin home, singing from the moment she crossed the threshold. A joyful memory struck: her eight-year-old self, dancing in the living room with Aunt Celia as Frank Sinatra's sonorous voice enticed her through the speakers, while her mother, who shared none of her older sister's *joie de vivre*, yelled at them both to stop that awful racket.

She wanted, God, how she wanted, to be a part of it. New York, New York!

Of course, her aunt would be changed, though how much she didn't know. Marie had mentioned their aunt's increasing cognitive decline while also assuring Jean that Aunt Celia was well-cared for and had little sense of time anymore, so Jean shouldn't feel guilty about not visiting. Marie had become increasingly reticent to talk about their aunt. Jean wondered how long it had been since Marie herself had visited, but she felt uncomfortable asking. Marie had done so much more for Aunt Celia than Jean had. The last thing she wanted to do was say anything that might be construed as criticism. When Jean finally made the move to Manhattan, Marie suggested they visit Aunt Celia together, but as much as Jean appreciated her cousin, she wanted time alone with their aunt. She hadn't even told Marie she was going to see her today. She would follow up with her cousin afterward.

Did Aunt Celia still dye her hair black, still pile on the makeup and costume jewelry, somehow managing to look fabulously eccentric but never tacky? Jean hoped so. Inspired by her aunt, Jean had prepared for her own New York adventure by getting rid of her gray, dying her hair a rich auburn. She had started wearing lipstick again and exchanged her sneakers for trim leather boots, her shapeless corduroys for fashionable high-waisted blue jeans, her drab sweatshirt for a jacket the color of bright red maple leaves that made her happy every time she put it on. At the airport before her flight, her daughter, Sabina, had hugged her with tears in her eyes and told Jean she looked beautiful. There was no higher praise than that.

A screeching sound combined with an indecipherable overhead announcement interrupted her reminiscing. Her train had pulled into Far Rockaway-Mott Avenue, the last stop. Jean stood and exited along with all the other passengers, including the off-duty MTA worker, whose eye she briefly caught. Part of her wanted to thank him for his kindness, but she suspected that would only advertise to those around her that she wasn't from these parts. None of the other passengers who had witnessed this man's selfless act acknowledged him, nor did he seem to seek any communication. So, she walked past him with only a brief nod and appreciative smile, at which he raised his eyebrows, looking startled, making her wish she had ignored him completely.

2

A VISIT WITH AUNT CELIA

Out on the crowded street, Jean opened her Google Maps app and followed the path indicated by the little blue dots on her screen, which took her down narrow, congested sidewalks. Construction seemed to be everywhere. Trucks and mashed-up concrete filled the streets. Dust choked the air.

Although she considered herself a New Yorker now, the Midwesterner within her still carried a fearfulness of New York City. As she walked, Jean worried that someone hurrying by her was going to snatch her phone right out of her hand. She really should put it in her purse. But then, how would she know where to go? She had no sense of direction, none.

On the back of her phone, a plastic pocket held her Metro card, bank cards, and driver's license. Oh, God. If someone snatched her phone right now, she was going to be royally screwed. How would she even get back on the subway? Did she have any cash in her wallet? She couldn't remember, and she wasn't going to check now. That would be an invitation for someone to steal her wallet as well as her phone.

Once again, Jean's heart pounded, and she gasped for air. Yes, she was beginning a new chapter in her life, but apparently, there were still going to be days when panic threatened to overwhelm her. She stopped walking, pressed her hand to her chest, and looked around her.

Breathe. Breathe.

A flash of orange caught her eye. There, a half-block ahead of her, was the man from the subway. He didn't hold a phone in his hand. This was a man who knew where he was going. How kind and gentle he'd been with that troubled woman on the train.

Jean passed a quaint little church on her left, white clapboard, blue trim, simple cross on the steeple. It would not have looked out of place in Baraboo, but seemed to have been plopped down in the wrong century here. It now sat looking strangely anachronistic amid the brick storefronts and chain-link fences. And on the right side of the street, letters of a different alphabet marked one sign after another. Hebrew perhaps? She'd passed several men wearing yarmulkes. Also, women wearing thick brown wigs, pushing strollers, and shepherding groups of as many as five children along. There were other women in hijabs and teenagers with ear buds and backpacks, and people in wheelchairs trying to navigate the treacherous street crossings. A can-do spirit emanated from them all.

She loved New York. She loved this sunny October day, this clear blue sky, warm yet crisp air, this gentle breeze with its unfamiliar tang of sea salt and tar. She loved the murmur of languages she didn't recognize, snatches of music she didn't know. She loved that New York was such a walkable city, that she and all her fellow New Yorkers could get practically anywhere by public transportation and good, honest walking. Jean could stand still and watch people walk past her all day long and never be bored. But of course, she couldn't, because she, like everyone else in this town, had somewhere she needed to be. She pushed back her shoulders, smiled, and started walking again.

The streets widened as she entered a more residential area, following those comforting blue dots, which guided her to the left here and to the right here. How would she have ever found her way before GPS? She could still see, a full block ahead of her now, the man with the orange vest. Wouldn't it be amusing if it turned out they were headed to the same place? If so, would he have any idea that they'd spent an hour riding in the same subway car? He was a memorable person, with his powerful build, assertive stride, and official looking orange vest, and those silver sprinkles in his dark hair, and his kind, tired eyes.

She was not a memorable person. When explaining why he didn't love her anymore, Todd said she'd let herself get drab and given up on her dreams and he didn't even know who she was. It still hurt because it felt so unfair—especially when he was the one who had quashed any of her attempts to follow those dreams. Like when she'd taken a painting class at the local art center and had wanted to claim just one small corner of the basement for her easel and paints. Todd refused to consolidate any of his sports equipment, bikes, golf clubs, rackets, skis, snowshoes. When she demanded to know why, he said he wasn't going to collude with her delusion that she had any talent, and that this hobby was worth her spending her time on. So, she'd dropped the class, stopped advocating for herself and instead, settled for being a martyr, overworked, unappreciated, self-sacrificial.

She couldn't bear to be around that person she'd become, either.

No more.

In what was turning out to be quite a pretty neighborhood, Jean turned down another residential street. She walked past a school with a brightly colored jungle gym in the courtyard, and here she was, already at the Sunset Care Nursing Residence, a one-story structure that took up half the block. It had taken her twelve years to get here, but she was here. One-thirty on the dot, no less.

She entered the lobby and had the immediate sensation of stepping backward in time. Several older adults sat in wheelchairs all grouped around the front desk. One man sang along to a Beatles song playing on a portable disk player. How long had it been since she'd seen one of those? A woman with long gray hair parked her wheelchair in front of what looked like an old-fashioned pay phone, which hung low to the ground, wheelchair height. It could pass for a museum piece, but the woman appeared to be talking on it. The receptionist, a stern older woman with a formidable square jaw, sat at the front desk, observing Jean with an expression of distrust.

"Jean Dennin," she announced herself with a cheery smile. "I called ahead. I'm here to visit my aunt, Celia Gruben."

She signed in, as directed, while the woman at the desk placed a call and spoke quietly into the phone. "She's not quite ready yet," she told Jean.

"I'm happy to go to her room," Jean said. "I can help her get ready."

"No. We'll bring her out. Just wait here."

Jean looked around the lobby. There were no seats. On the other side of a large window, she saw an appealing terrace with one large and several small circular tables, which sat unoccupied. "Would it be possible for me to sit out there?" she asked.

"It's not open," the receptionist said.

Jean counted eight people in wheelchairs in the hallway, looking out the glass windows at the patio. Longingly, she suspected.

"It's a lovely day out," she said.

"You may wait in the recreation room." The woman pressed her lips together, no doubt cognizant of Jean's understated criticism. "First right down that hallway."

"Oh, okay. She'll be out soon?"

The receptionist offered a tight smile and said nothing. Jean walked to the recreation room, a dark room with four rectangular brown tables. At one, a woman with gray, curly hair, perhaps sixty, sat beside a much older man in a wheelchair. They were playing cards. How sweet. Maybe she was his daughter or even his niece. Jean walked to the table farthest from the door, brushed crumbs off one of the seats, and sat down. After ten minutes, she took out her novel and read a few pages. Then a woman approached her.

"I'm sorry. I'm going to have to ask you to wait in the lobby," she said. "I'm the recreation director here and I'm about to run a program."

"Oh," said Jean. "The woman at the front desk told me to wait here."

"You'll need to go back to the front desk, I'm afraid," the woman said politely.

"Is there any chance I could sit out on the patio?"

"It isn't open."

"I see that." Jean dug her fingernails into her palms, forcing herself to keep smiling. "But could it be opened? It's a beautiful day out. Not too cold. Perhaps some of the residents would enjoy it."

"We open it at two."

Jean looked at her phone. Just ten minutes more then. And wouldn't that be nice to sit out there on that pretty patio with Aunt Celia? She went back to the front lobby and leaned against a wall. The Beatles fan held his portable disk player in his lap and sang along to "Hey, Jude." Ten minutes passed. A staff member opened the patio and the residents in the hallway wheeled themselves outside. Jean stayed where she was. Twenty minutes. Thirty. At 2:30 p.m., Jean approached the front desk.

"Could you give me some idea of when my aunt might be

coming out?"

"She was asleep," the woman said. "Then she was giving them a hard time. They're getting her dressed now. Soon."

Way down the hall, a tall, broad man wheeled a thin, lanky man toward the patio. No orange vest, yet she wondered if this was her subway companion. She peered from below her lashes, trying not to be obvious. It was, she was certain. What were the odds of that? He was here, visiting someone he cared about, his father, or uncle, or old friend, just like she was. He backed into the glass door and pulled the wheelchair through to the patio, then settled himself and the elderly man at a table directly in the warm sun.

Soon, she would be out there too. Maybe the four of them would strike up a conversation. Jean smiled and shook her head at herself. Hadn't life taught her nothing good could come from such foolish fantasies? And yet, the fact that she had developed a little crush on a complete stranger (though oddly, he didn't feel like a stranger anymore) stirred some tiny spark of hope within her. She wasn't completely washed up, after all.

An aide wheeled a tiny, white-haired woman in a wheelchair into the lobby. Jean glanced at the woman, who stared straight in front of her. Jean peered down the hallway again. This was taking forever. She'd been waiting for over an hour.

Then she noticed both the aide and the receptionist watching her, expecting something from her. Uneasily, she looked again at the woman in the wheelchair who had just arrived. The woman glanced at her and then looked away.

Jean stared. This couldn't be Aunt Celia, could it? This vacant-looking woman in a gray cardigan, thin white hair, no makeup, no jewelry, no light in her eyes, no smile.

"Is this Celia Gruben?" Jean asked.

The aide raised an eyebrow and nodded. "What is your relationship to her?"

"I'm her niece, Jean Dennin."

"You're not listed in her file."

"No, I'm sure my cousin Marie Vest is listed. I lived in the Midwest until recently. This is my first time visiting her here." At the mention of Marie's name, both the aide and the receptionist relaxed, as if they'd been suspicious of her.

Jean crouched by the wheelchair. Well, she supposed this could be her aunt. It must be. They would hardly bring out some other woman to test her. And yes, there was that dark little mole under Celia's right eye. Thank God, an identifying mark! She smiled at her aunt, hoping for some glimmer of recognition in the woman's eyes, but Aunt Celia returned her cheery gaze with a look of utter boredom before closing her eyes and turning her head to the side.

"She was napping," the aide said.

"May I take her out to the terrace?" Jean asked.

The aide nodded, and Jean followed her outside. The aide parked Aunt Celia's chair by the one empty table. "Bring her back to the front desk when you're ready to leave and they'll call me," the aide said.

At a larger table near the wall, the recreation leader was now running a bingo game with six participants. Several other residents sat in their chairs facing the manicured lawn, enjoying the sun. Jean spotted "the man with the orange vest," as she'd come to think of him, sitting at the table adjacent to theirs. He was holding up an iPad showing a video of a baby elephant taking a bath in a small plastic pool. The old man beside him laughed with delight, tears rolling gently down his leathery cheeks. What a good idea to bring some kind of entertainment. She wished she'd thought of that.

Jean sat beside her aunt and beamed at her. "Aunt Celia," she began.

The woman's eyes remained closed. She gave no response.

Jean blinked back tears. Marie had told her that Aunt Celia wasn't as communicative as she used to be. That was an understatement. Aunt Celia didn't seem to recognize her at all. And Jean had wanted so much to be seen, once again, by this woman who had been so formative in her life. She supposed she should have known how unrealistic her longing had been, but she had hoped nevertheless.

Still, however changed, this was the aunt who had adored her, and whom Jean had adored in return. Perhaps she could bring her some comfort, some pleasure. Music was supposed to be one of the longest lasting memories. In a soft voice, Jean hummed the tune to "New York, New York," the song they had danced to and sung together so many times over the years. Nothing. No response whatsoever. Jean leaned forward and quietly sang the words. Her aunt glanced at her a couple of times, lips flattened together, her face expressionless.

At least she seemed able to hear. So, she would speak to her.

"You taught me that song, Aunt Celia," she said. "Do you remember? I used to look forward to your visits to Wisconsin so much. You would sweep through our front door with your arms full of packages for us. You brought the best presents. I still have that darling little jewelry box you gave me, with all the cubbyholes for my earrings. You used to wear bright red lipstick and lots of rouge. Mother thought it was too much rouge, but I liked it. I thought you were the most beautiful woman I'd ever seen. And the most fun. Your visits brightened up summer like nothing else."

She stared at her aunt, whose eyes had closed again. Her own eyes were wet. Blinking rapidly, she turned her head, just in time to see the man from the subway turning away. Had he been watching her? Why did he suddenly seem so grim?

Oh, what did it matter? She couldn't focus on what some strange man might think of her. She turned back to her aunt.

"I'm sorry it's been so long, Aunt Celia. I really am. It didn't work out with me and Todd. I guess you were right about him, but at least I have my kids, and they're wonderful. You haven't seen them since they were little, I know. The last few years have been hard. My parents both got so sick. You wouldn't have recognized your little sister at the end. I'm sorry that she just didn't have the energy to keep up with you on the phone. Anyway, I won't bore you with all the details. It's just been hard, that's all. Not the happiest years of my life, to put it mildly. No, that was probably childhood, and you had a lot to do with making those years happy."

Jean's eyes teared again, looking at the unresponsive woman in the chair beside her. She leaned forward. "Aunt Celia, thank you for everything you did to make my childhood magical, at least for little bursts of time during the summer and at Christmas when you would visit from New York. I can't tell you how much that meant to me. You took me to the Firehouse Fairs in the summer. Do you remember those? With the rides? We would ride the carousel together. You always wanted to be on a blue horse. You said the blue horses were lucky. And you bought me cotton candy, as long as I promised not to tell my mother, which I never did. It was our secret. And you taught me so many songs."

Aunt Celia raised her head and watched Jean, her lips still in a flat line. Was anything getting through? Any memories being stirred? Could she at least tell that she was looking at someone who loved and appreciated her? Oh, God, her poor aunt, come to this! A shell of the woman she had been. No, she mustn't think those thoughts, lest her pity and outright dismay broadcast itself from her face. Another song, then. Her aunt was in there somewhere. Some song would prove to be the key that would bring her aunt to herself, at least for a moment. Oh, yes!

"Aunt Celia, do you remember this one? You would sing it to

me at bedtime: 'When Irish eyes are smiling, sure it's like a morn in spring. In the lilt of Irish laughter, you can hear the angels sing. When Irish hearts are happy, all the world seems bright and gay…'"

"Would you shut up!" Aunt Celia snapped. "For God's sake, shut up with that singing!"

Jean's mouth clamped shut. She jerked back in her chair. She could feel the color draining from her face. What just happened?

Did her aunt, her beloved aunt, really just tell her to shut up? Her aunt had never, never spoken to her in such a tone before. She'd certainly never told her to stop singing.

"Aunt Celia!"

"You'll pay for this. You will learn. I'll make sure of it!" Aunt Celia glared at her. Then she tried to spit at her, though, fortunately, no spittle came out.

Jean's breath stuck in her throat. Her fists clenched so hard she knew her fingernails were making imprints on her palms, though she didn't feel pain.

"Do you know who I am?" Jean asked softly.

"I don't know, and I don't care." Her aunt's icy blue eyes held Jean's gaze with a venomous glare. "It's too late. That ship has sailed. Where do you get your big ideas from? Think you're so special, don't you? You should know better. Stop that awful racket."

My God. Jean's heart pounded. Aunt Celia sounded just like Jean's mother. And just like her dour grandmother.

The rest of the patio had grown quiet. Everyone around them, everyone who could hear anyway, had heard the way her aunt just spoke to her. Jean focused her eyes on her lap, hurt and humiliated. What was she supposed to do now? Leave after fifteen minutes of trying to talk to the aunt she hadn't seen in twelve years?

Behind her, she heard indecipherable mumbling followed by a high-pitched, wheezy laugh. A quick glance over her shoulder let her see that the hero of the A train was showing the old man another humorous video, this one of a mother bear trying to cross a highway with four cubs. She loved that video. She tried to catch the younger man's eye, hoping for a sympathetic smile. He wasn't smiling at all as he shifted in his chair, turning his back to her.

Well, so much for a possible connection between them. The last thing she needed in her life was another hypercritical, disapproving, sour-faced person to make her feel small and worthless. Who was he to judge her? Jean returned her gaze to her lap, trying to squelch her profound disappointment with him, with her aunt, with this whole miserable day.

Oh God. She was mortified. All her happy thoughts on the way out here had burst like soap bubbles, her delightful fantasy of a joyful reunion with her aunt, and her tiny, barely voiced fantasy that this seemingly decent, handsome man would see her do something kind for another human being.

Jean sat there, utterly flummoxed as to what to do next, and just plain sad. The woman who had once been her Aunt Celia, though she bore almost no resemblance to the aunt Jean had adored, truly did not know who she was. However guilty Jean felt over her long absence, she knew her aunt's behavior was not intentional, certainly not meant to punish any perceived negligence. Her aunt would never have wanted to hurt her this way. Was this why Marie had repeatedly suggested they make this visit together? After all Jean had been through with her divorce and her sick parents, had her sweet cousin been trying to protect her from one more heartbreak?

But Jean wasn't ready to give up yet. Even though the subway hero had seemed disapproving of her, he had given her a good idea for how to get through to her aunt. She took out her phone and pulled up a YouTube video of Frank Sinatra singing "New York, New York" at a concert in Tokyo in 1985 and played it at a low volume. Aunt Celia, whose eyes were now shut again, nodded her head once, twice, three times. Possibly to the music? It was hard to say.

"Aunt Celia?"

Her aunt lunged forward in her seat and threw out one of her skinny arms as if trying to hit Jean. "You should know better. It's too late for this shit. You really think you're something, don't you? Well, take it from me. You're not." She sat back in her seat, fixed Jean with a malevolent glare for a long moment, and then closed her eyes and dropped her head.

Jean's body trembled. Sweat dampened her armpits. Nausea roiled her stomach.

All right, God, just get me out of this building. Please.

If Jean hadn't been so aware of Mr. MTA sitting so still at the next table, face averted, silently judging her, she might well have dashed from the patio, down the hall, through the lobby, out the front doors, never to return. But he was there, and though why in the world it should matter to her that he not see her run away, it did matter. She'd show him what she was made of. She stood, walked behind her aunt's wheelchair, and tried to pull it away from the table. The chair wouldn't move.

Breathe.

"You need to unlock the brake, honey," said a young aide near her, who had been scrolling through her phone while her charge, an extremely thin old woman, dozed in the sunlight.

Right. The brake. She knew that. How many times had she wheeled her own father around in a wheelchair similar to this one? She could do this.

"Thank you," she murmured. She studiously avoided looking at the man from the subway, afraid of what she might see in his eyes if he glanced in her direction—pity, scorn, even?

These brakes worked differently from the ones on her father's old wheelchair, but eventually, she figured out how to release them. She pulled the chair back through the glass doors and down the hall to the front desk.

"That's it?" the square-jawed woman at the front desk asked, with genuine surprise.

"Well, it takes me two and a half hours to get home from here," Jean said. "I live in Inwood."

The woman raised an eyebrow and picked up her phone. "I'll call her aide then."

Jean waited until she hung up the phone. "Is there anyone I could speak to about my aunt's condition? I'm just wondering if today was a typical day or... it's just that she was quite different from how I remember her."

"You're not on the list of people we can share information with," the woman at the desk said. "If you can get your cousin Marie to add your name, then we could talk with you."

Jean nodded. "Oh, right. Of course. I understand," and then, "Thank you for taking good care of her," she said to the aide, who took her place behind the wheelchair. She meant that. Aunt Celia was obviously clean, her clothes were neat and tidy, her hair was washed, her fingernails clipped.

"You might try visiting in the morning," the aide said softly, not wanting to be overheard.

Jean felt a glimmer of hope. "Oh. Okay. Thank you. I'll talk to Marie, too. Yes. Thank you." She braced herself, preparing for another tongue lashing, and crouched down far enough away so that her aunt couldn't reach her if she tried to swing her arms. "Goodbye, Aunt Celia. It was lovely to see you again."

"Lovely to see you too, dear," Aunt Celia said, her eyes half-closed.

The aide shrugged, smiling, and pushed her aunt back down the hall.

3

A WALK ON THE BEACH

Jean walked out of the building, stood on the sidewalk, and made herself take a deep breath, then another, then another. She didn't know where to go or what to do, so she just stood there, feeling sad and weary, letting the minutes pass.

"Excuse me." A deep voice sounded behind her.

She knew exactly who it was and if he thought she was going to tolerate any scolding words from him... Suddenly, all the emotions piling up within her from this whole horrible day spilled over and she burst into tears.

"What?" she cried, turning to face him. "It's not enough for you to turn your back on me when you know nothing about my relationship with my aunt, but now you have something you need to say to me, too?"

He took a step back, lifting his hands in a defensive gesture, his eyes wide with surprise.

They stood facing each other in silence. Jean sniffed and wiped the back of her hand under her nose, the tears still flowing. She tried to keep glaring at him, but found she couldn't, not when looking into those gentle brown eyes. She blinked through her tears, willing them to stop.

The man slowly lowered his hands. He tilted his head, as if curious or concerned. "Hey. I was just trying to give you some privacy there and keep my dad from adding any fuel to the fire. He was wanting to jump into your conversation, and believe me, that isn't something you would have enjoyed."

Jean pulled some tissues from her purse and wiped her eyes and nose. Oh, what in the world was wrong with her? Had he actually been trying to be considerate, and she'd just bitten his head off?

"I couldn't help overhearing you," he continued. "I could see how hard you were trying to reach your aunt and how much she meant to you. And I could tell how upsetting your conversation was. So, I just wanted to say that I'm sorry you had such a hard time in there. That's all."

Jean nodded, crumpling the damp tissues and shoving them back into her purse. "And somehow I haven't managed to scare you off?"

He smiled and shook his head. "I don't scare easy."

They eyed each other for another moment before Jean allowed herself to return his smile. "I'm so sorry. It felt like the whole world was against me in there."

"Some days are like that." He jutted his chin toward the street. "I usually take a little walk on the beach after I visit my father and I just wondered...." He pointed in the opposite direction from which they'd come. "I heard you say you're from Wisconsin. Have you ever seen the beach?"

"I've seen the beach on Lake Michigan," she said.

"What about the ocean?" he asked.

She shook her head.

"Well, if you have time, it's worth seeing. This isn't the prettiest beach down this end, but it's still a beach."

"How far will it take me from the subway station? I need to get back home at some point. Are you going back to the station too? I'm Jean, by the way. We were on the same car on the A train."

"Chuck. And, yeah, I know we were."

He held out his hand in an oddly formal gesture, and she shook it. Was it her imagination that he seemed to hold on to hers for a beat too long? Yet, as she pulled away, it wasn't her imagination to see a wedding ring on his finger. Oh, well.

"No, I'm not going back to the station," Chuck said. "I live out here. But I'm happy to walk you there after the beach. It doesn't add much to the walk going this way."

"Okay. But you've already done your good deed for the day. Three good deeds, actually. Helping that troubled woman on the train, and visiting your father, and being sympathetic to me. What were you worried your father was going to do? He seemed like a sweet old man."

"Yeah," Chuck said, ambling down the sidewalk. She fell into step beside him. "He is a sweet old man now, most of the time, though he was a royal son of a bitch for most of my life. He's actually had a clash or two with your aunt before and man, when they get into it with each other, it's not pretty. I was worried about a blowup between them from the minute you sat down near our table and as soon as your aunt started yelling at you, my dad perked up like he wanted to join in. Fortunately, I was able to distract him."

"The bears."

He nodded. "Bears to the rescue, every time."

"It seems like you have a warm relationship with him now."

Chuck shrugged. "I guess I can consider it a blessing that I get to see a gentler side of him before he dies. Makes me wonder if he was like that when he was a little boy. Or maybe that side of him stayed locked away his whole life until all his defenses finally came down. Who knows?"

"That is truly terrifying," Jean said.

"How so?" He guided her across a double lane highway and pointed out the direction they were heading.

"My aunt was one of the most loving people I've ever known, and I always wanted to be like her. Sweet and hopeful and adventurous. But maybe she was hiding rage her whole life. Like I do. I'm so angry about so many things. I try to hide it, because who wants to see that, you know? Even I don't. Life is too short. But it's there, and someday, I'll probably have lost my mind and be stuck out in some place like that, saying horrible things to my children or anyone else who tries to be nice to me. Though I hope my children don't abandon me the way I abandoned her."

After a few moments of quiet walking, Chuck said, "I wasn't eavesdropping on purpose, but I couldn't help overhearing that you had a lot of other responsibilities keeping you in Wisconsin, so I'm not sure it's fair to you to say you abandoned her. I can relate to the guilt, though. When my wife got sick, the last year especially, I didn't get out here much to see my dad, even though I was a lot closer than Wisconsin. You can only do what you can do, you know?"

She glanced at his wedding ring. "Is your wife... did she...?"

He nodded. "Two years ago." He lifted his left hand, looking at his ring. "My kids keep telling me it's time to take this off, but... I don't know. Soon, maybe." Tears rose to his eyes. He blinked them away.

"Don't rush it."

They walked in silence for a few minutes. Then he cleared his throat. "You know it's not your fault that she was mean like that, don't you?"

"I wish you hadn't heard her," Jean said.

He shrugged. "No choice. Everyone heard her. Everyone who could hear, anyway, so not everyone." He smiled.

Jean sighed. "I don't think it's my fault. I honestly don't know what I could have done differently. I took care of my parents at home, and I couldn't get away. But maybe, if I had been able to visit, she wouldn't have forgotten me so completely." They walked in silence, heading toward a boardwalk that she could see, with sand behind it, and long grasses. Despite herself, she lifted her chin and smiled. "The beach!"

"That's it." Chuck grinned at her. "And by the way, forgive me if I'm jumping to a conclusion here, but I think maybe you think you're more powerful than you actually are. Nothing you did or didn't do could make someone behave that way, you know? Dementia is just cruel. Like mental illness, like that poor lady on the train. Or, I should say, dementia can be cruel. In my case, it's actually been kind, but I couldn't make my dad be sweet any more than you can make your aunt be vicious. Life is just strange that way. How's that for a profound observation?"

He laughed at himself, and Jean couldn't help but laugh too.

"It's windy," she said as they stepped onto the boardwalk. Between sand dunes, she could see the sandy beach and slate gray waves crashing gently on the shore.

"I usually walk on the beach itself, but we don't have to if you don't want to scuff up your boots," Chuck said.

"I think walking on the beach would be worth a few scuffs on my boots." Jean followed him onto the sand, which was more unwieldy than it looked like, and made walking difficult, though she didn't care. She enjoyed the challenge. "I love this smell. I wish I could bottle it!" The wind whipped her hair across her face.

"Nothing like sea air and salt water. It's cleansing."

"Do you swim here?" She stopped walking, suddenly aware of shells covering the sand all around them. She squatted down and picked up a broken clam shell.

"In the summer, yeah. There are better beaches for swimming, though." He handed her an unbroken clam shell. "Here. You can start a collection."

"Thank you." She closed her fingers around the shell. "I better not collect any more today, though. I can see myself not getting very far down the beach. Wow, look at all these shells! They're beautiful."

Reluctantly, she stood, put her hand to her forehead to keep her hair from her eyes, and grinned at Chuck.

He'd been watching her, she realized. He gave an embarrassed smile and turned away. His strides were long. She hurried to catch up with him.

"How cold do you think the water is?" she asked.

"Might be cold," he said. "After all, it's October, though in September it's still nice."

"I want to try putting my feet in the water. Is that really stupid?"

He shook his head.

She sat down, unlaced her boots, and took off her socks. "I promise I'll keep my pants on, don't worry," she said as she rolled up her pant legs. Listening to her own words, her cheeks heated. "I was referring to the woman on the subway," she explained, suddenly afraid to look up at him.

"I know," he said, and his amused, nonjudgmental voice instantly calmed her. He reached out a hand to help her stand. She hesitated, then took it, offering a quick smile of thanks.

Then she made her way to the dark, damp sand. "Yikes! It is cold! I can feel it on the sand." She laughed, standing still for a moment. Then she ran toward the water and stood until a tiny wave spilled over her toes. "It's so cold!" she wailed, stamping her feet, and turning to Chuck with a smile so wide her cheeks hurt. She turned back to the water and took a step forward. "Come again, waves!" she cried. "I can stand it!"

Another wave covered both her feet and this time she didn't cry out at all. She was getting acclimated. The wind and her hair whipped her face, making her eyes tear, and then she was crying again.

"Hey, Jean." Chuck moved to her side, letting his shoes get wet. "Are you okay?"

She nodded. "I'm okay," she said, wiping her face. "I think I'm happy. I don't know for sure. It's been so long. Thank you for bringing me out here. Thank you for being part of this day. I can't tell you how grateful I am that we were on the same subway car together and I got to see you be a hero to that woman. And then you were so sweet to me after that disaster with my aunt, even after I snapped at you. Really, the whole day would have been so much worse without you." She noticed he was holding her boots, with her socks stuffed inside, with one hand. "Oops. Thanks, I'll take those."

She reached for them, but he didn't hand them over. Instead, he stopped in front of her, put a gentle finger under her chin, and lifted her face to his.

"Jean," he said, as though he liked the sound of her name. And then he smiled—a smile that lit his whole face—and for the first time all day, his eyes seemed lively, twinkling, not tired at all. "You made my day better, too."

FIRE

Boy

A Pine Lodge Tale

1

STORMY NIGHT

It was a dark and stormy night, all right. Another hour on these treacherous Adirondack roads would just about do her in. Not to mention her poor 14-year-old Honda, inherited from her beloved grandmother, which Heidi Pfeiffer intended to drive until it fell apart. Alan used to be so embarrassed to have the neighbors see his fiancée in this ancient car. What a relief that she no longer had to give a shit about his obsession with appearances. She loved the car, okay? He liked his fancy new cars, she liked her battered-up old car. And she did not consider that a character flaw.

Heidi gritted her teeth. Why was she still rehearsing this stupid argument in her head? The last time they'd quarreled about this in person was eighteen months ago. He was married, for goodness' sake, to prissy Angela, who drove a spiffy new car, which must make him so proud. Alan's control issues were not her problem anymore.

Yet, she still felt that she was learning from scratch how to breathe again. That's what nine straight years of suffocation would do to you.

What the heck was the deal with the streetlights? As in, why weren't they on? Bad enough that it was pouring, and the roads full of potholes and puddles, but relying only on her headlights for sight, Heidi really did feel like she was searching for a pine needle in a forest of towering pines.

Her anticipated six-hour drive to Pine Lodge was going on eleven hours at this point. She'd counted on her GPS to get her there. She had not counted on getting no cell phone reception. Or on her phone battery dying. Finally, she found a gas station that sold maps, those ancient relics. Then her spatial relations skills, which had never been all that functional, went completely AWOL.

She would never have found herself in this situation had she been traveling with Alan. He would have planned out the entire trip down to the last mile. He would have memorized the weather forecast for each segment of the journey. He would never have been surprised by a torrential rainstorm or the possibility that they might not have cell phone reception. He would have known exactly what to expect and been prepared for all eventualities. If she had been traveling with Alan, she would have arrived at this new job at a decent daylight hour. *What kind of first impression do you think you're going to make on your new employers, Heidi, showing up for work smack in the middle of the night?*

Oh, shut up, Alan! It's not a character flaw to get lost once in a while either, for goodness' sake.

In fact, there was something almost exhilarating about having gotten not just lost, but so completely lost that for a couple hours there she really hadn't had any idea where she was. And yet, she was still okay. Nothing fundamentally terrible had happened to her. And eventually, she'd found herself heading in the right direction. See, Alan? Not the end of the world, after all.

Oh, God, it was so good to be free!

Of course, she would feel even better if he didn't hate her guts, but she'd brought that on herself. She was going to have to live with her guilt and his hate for the rest of her life. It was a heavy weight, but not as heavy a weight as the relationship had been.

She had to be almost there. In fact, the skyline seemed to be clearing. For the first time in what felt like forever, she saw the outlines of buildings. Her headlights lit up a sign: *Pine Lodge: Welcome to Your Home in the Woods.*

Well, praise the Lord, as her grandmother would say. Two AM, according to her watch. Mrs. Hodges had told her someone would wait up for her if she arrived late. The darkened building, a large, brown, clapboard house, which she figured must be the main lodge, suggested otherwise. Not even a candle in a window.

Warm welcome, check.

Heidi pulled into what she thought might be a parking space and turned off the engine, though she left her lights on, so she could get the lay of the land. "We made it here alive. That's what matters," she muttered, patting the dash of her Honda.

She peered out the car's windows, which were still being splattered with rain. Behind her, she could just make out a square, two-story building that she guessed had some kind of utilitarian function. Garage maybe? Time would tell. The main lodge seemed to be at the top of a gentle hill that sloped down to a lake. White Pine Lake, she remembered. To her left, through the trees, she saw a couple of cabins by the water, trickles of smoke drifting out of the chimneys. She wondered where the staff stayed. Not too far away, she hoped. She was so tired.

Pulling up the hood of her windbreaker, she opened her car door and stepped first one foot and then another into an ankle-deep puddle. She let the water soak through her sneakers. She had no energy left to protest. It was just that kind of night.

Could be worse.

Something she actually didn't want to consider as she stood there up to her ankles in muddy water in the middle of the night, torrential rain pouring down on her. Looking at the outlines of unlit buildings. Seeing no other cars in the parking lot. Hearing no signs of human life. A shiver ran up her spine. This place was creepy.

Okay. This moment was really and truly not the time for a freak-out. She tried to let her eyes adjust to the darkness. Someone had to be here. Preferably someone alive. Who wasn't carrying an axe. After having escaped from a maximum-security prison for serial killers. "Not the time for a freak-out," she reminded herself through gritted teeth.

Lifting her water-logged feet, she traipsed through puddles to the building she thought must be the main lodge, and knocked on the side door. Hearing nothing, she turned the knob. The door opened for her.

Good security system, check.

Her sneakers squished as she shuffled into the dark room, arms stretched forward, until she knocked her hip against a chair. Groping, she discerned other chairs around a table. Worst-case scenario, she could sleep on one of those chairs. Moving a bit to the left, she discovered a counter, which she braced herself against.

"Hellooo. Hellooo." Her voice sounded strange in her ears. "This is Heidi. Is anybody here?"

An inarticulate, deep-throated shout sounded from upstairs. After a moment, feet pounded on the hall above her head and thudded down a staircase, which, from the sound of it, was on the opposite end of the room. Those heavy feet did not belong to Mrs. Wanda Hodges, that much Heidi knew. The person stopped at the bottom. Heidi pressed back against the counter.

Mystery man, check.

Now, instead of Alan's voice, she heard her parents: *What do you really know about the people who run this place, which no one we know has ever heard of? We understand you need to move out of our house, but you're sure you won't try to find a job closer to home? Remember that you are a young, single woman. It's a dangerous world out there. Do you really understand how vulnerable you are? Do you know how many inmates escape from prison every year in New York State alone? Rapists. Kidnappers. Murderers. Promise us you will always carry pepper spray.*

What do you mean you left it in the car?

Heidi gritted her teeth. *Shut up, Mom and Dad!*

Don't say we didn't warn you.

They were ridiculous! There was no reason to think this guy was anyone but the employee whose job it was to wait up for her. Still. There was also no reason not to take precautions. Her hands searched the surface for some kind of weapon and grasped what had to be a pencil.

"Is anyone actually here or am I dreaming the new cook finally deigned to show up?" An arrogant male voice.

"Do you not use lights around here?" Heidi snapped, hoping anger covered the tremor in her voice.

"Power's out."

"I tried to call over and over until my phone died. No one ever bothered to answer."

"Phone lines must be down."

"Oh. Okay." She wanted to add that she was soaking wet and bone tired, but she had a feeling he wouldn't be interested, whoever he was. An employee, she hoped, not an escaped convict pretending to be an employee. She kept her back against the counter. Her hand tightened around the pencil. She wished she could see something. Anything. It seemed darker inside than outside.

"Sorry to be grumpy. Just my assignment to wait up for you

and I fell asleep. It's okay. I have to get up in a couple hours, anyway. I'm Doug Barrett, fire boy, at your service."

He sounded normal enough.

"Fire boy? What does that mean? Professional arsonist?"

"Exactly."

"Really?"

"No."

"Ha ha. Okay, then. What does a fire boy do?"

He remained at the foot of the staircase. She thought she heard him sitting down. Her racing heart began to slow its pace.

"I keep the cabin fires lit." His voice seemed tired, but calm. "And chop wood."

She was convinced: he really worked here. "Okay, fire boy. Is the power ever going to come back on?"

He paused for a moment before answering, "It always has."

Okay, that was probably a stupid question. She tried again. "Any chance of finding candles around here?"

"Yes. Even better: a kerosene lamp."

"Were you intending to light one?"

"I don't know. We seem to be managing okay here in the dark."

"It's Doug, right?"

"Right."

"You are obviously pissed that I'm so late. I'm sorry. I got completely lost. My GPS didn't work, and I got confusing directions and ended up at a place called Pine Wood Cabins. The couple who runs the place must have thought I was a lunatic. I kept insisting to them that they'd hired me to work through the summer and could they please show me my room."

Doug laughed. She liked his laugh. It was a rich, deep, surprisingly playful laugh. "Pine Wood Cabins. I know that place. Languid Lake, right? That's three hours away."

"Five hours by the route I took." She glanced out the window behind her. "Does it rain like this often?"

"This summer, yes. A real challenge for me finding a way to keep wood dry. Anyway, I'm happy to light the lantern, but it's on the counter behind you. You might be able to find it and the matches if you feel around."

"You don't want to light it yourself?"

"I don't know. Are you still afraid I'm going to do nefarious things to you?"

"What?" Had she been that obvious? "I'm not afraid."

"Are you sure?" The sound of knees cracking indicated he was now standing again. "Because you seem really on edge, and I am really not in the mood to get attacked if you suddenly decide I'm a threat."

"You're worried about getting attacked?" she cried, astonished. "Don't be ridiculous! If anyone has to worry about being attacked in this situation, it's me." The minute the words left her mouth, she clamped her lips shut, embarrassed. She was channeling her parents and their worries. This man wasn't going to attack her. If anything, she had somewhat enjoyed the back-and-forth banter they'd been having.

To her chagrin, a marked silence followed. When he finally spoke, his tone was curt, as if she had offended him. "Actually, no," he said, "you really don't need to worry about being attacked."

"Sorry, Doug." She tried to make her voice sound teasing instead of nervous. "I'm a little jumpy. I honestly don't think you're going to attack me. I'm convinced you actually work here and haven't escaped from a maximum-security prison for serial killers."

Another silence, longer this time. So much for lightening things up. The mood felt charged now, more unsettled. Or maybe she was reading too much into this. She was very tired.

"Okay. Um." She cleared her throat. "I'm afraid we're getting off on the wrong foot here. Sorry if I've said anything to offend you. I was a little nervous, but I'm fine now. Go ahead. Get some light in here. Please."

"All right," he said, his tone both brusque and resigned.

A chair scraped against the floor as he made his way over. At the same time, something rubbed up against her leg, some living thing. Before she could stop herself, she shrieked at the top of her lungs.

"Stop! Oh, God, what is it?" she cried, as once again, the thing brushed against her leg.

He was at her side in a moment. Scrunching her arms to her chest, she pressed herself against this gruff, irritable man she'd just met and still hadn't seen, hoping for protection against the unknown living creature who was also in the room with them.

"What the hell?" He placed his hands on her hips and emphatically pushed her away from him. "Jesus! Calm down! What's the matter?"

"Oh, God!" Her whole body trembled. It took everything in her power not to ignore the very obvious message he'd just given that she needed to keep her distance from him. "Something touched me! What is that thing? Oh, no, it's touching me again!" she shrieked. "Help! Stop it!"

Doug leaned over and picked up a creature who meowed.

"Oh, my God!" She let out a deep breath, relieved and humiliated, still pressing her hands against her racing heart. "Oh, my God. It's a cat." She was officially mortified.

More footsteps pounded upstairs. "Hey, Doug," a male voice called. "Who are you slaughtering down there?"

Even in the dark, she could feel Doug stiffen beside her, radiating irritation. This guy was hypersensitive. Heidi had no idea who the man upstairs was, but she knew enough to be able to tell he was joking.

A beat later, however, Doug shouted back: "Our new cook, Heidi. I had to. She was another histrionic female, just like the last one."

"Excuse me?" Heidi asked, indignantly. She wasn't a hundred percent sure what histrionic meant, but it didn't sound like a compliment. And what the heck was the deal with this guy's vocabulary? He talked like a college professor, not a fire boy.

"She sounds alive," came the voice from above.

"She is," Doug admitted. "She just met Monster."

"Ah. Got it. 'Night." The footsteps overhead traipsed away.

"Heidi, Monster. Monster, Heidi." Doug leaned on the counter beside her, his warm arm just barely touching hers, and cuddled the cat. "He loves freaking out the staff. He thinks we're so funny when we scream."

That was kind of sweet. He could have mocked her or at least teased, but he didn't. She was freezing, but he exuded heat. She wanted to wrap herself around him, just to get warm, but he'd already made it clear he didn't like being touched. Regretfully, she moved over an inch, losing the heat from his arm. She could sense him relaxing as he stood there, holding the cat.

"Has he ever made you scream?" she asked.

"Every morning of my first two weeks on the job. He deposits trophies on my pillow. Chipmunk heads, squirrel tails, bird carcasses. I never know what will be the first thing I see when I open my eyes in the morning. This guy is a real predator, aren't you, Monster?"

He made kissy noises at the cat. The cat purred.

Okay, she really needed to see this guy's face. He was a complete enigma: grumpy, easily offended, yet capable of humor and sweetness—to a cat, at least.

"What made him stop?"

"Stop what? Oh. He hasn't stopped. I've just built up my tolerance for animal gore. No more screaming."

Heidi swallowed, feeling almost faint. "Am I sleeping in this house?" Waking up to a chipmunk head on her pillow would knock her smack over the edge.

All of a sudden, she feared she was not going to be able to handle this whole situation. She couldn't bear the possibility of her parents being right. They understood that she had to get out of Mapleton, where she'd spent the past year and more with an invisible "A" practically branded on her chest. But they had urged her to look for work closer to home, and more in line with the kind of job they considered suitable, like the nice, staid office job she'd had until last year, working as a receptionist in Alan's family's financial services business. They didn't care for her more recent job at Angie's Restaurant. Why work in a hot kitchen around all that messy food when she could sit behind a nice sterile desk and answer phones?

No, her parents would never understand her.

Tears pricked her eyes. But she couldn't, she just could not cry in front of this guy who already thought she was a total nutcase.

"No, you're not staying here." She sensed a smile and gentleness in his voice. "Girls—women, I mean, sleep above the Laundry. Behind where you probably parked your car. I'm pretty sure there's no cat hanging out over there depositing goodies or I would have heard about it by now. Hold him?"

Doug placed Monster in Heidi's arms and fumbled around on the counter. Monster's warm, purring body had a welcome, calming effect. A match lit, then a candle, and a kerosene lamp, which Doug held up to her face.

"You're so young," he said. "I'm surprised you have a driver's license. Are you in college?"

"I'm not that young," she snapped. If she'd heard that comment once, she'd heard it a thousand times.

His looks surprised her, too. With a scruffy dark beard and

mustache covering half his face and a wary expression in his gray-blue eyes, he looked older than she'd expected.

"You look twelve," he insisted. "But what big brown eyes you have."

"Thanks so much," she said sarcastically. "What big white teeth you have."

"The better to... never mind." He glanced at her with eyebrows raised, and she stared at him, her cheeks suddenly flushing with heat. He ran a hand through his thick dark hair and looked away, embarrassed. "Lost my train of thought. How old are you, anyway?"

"Twenty-seven," she said. "I finished college six years ago. And you?"

"Twenty-six. Starting college this fall. Late bloomer."

"Oh." She knew there must be a story behind that. Monster, who the lamp revealed to be a black cat with unnerving emer-ald-green eyes, squirmed in her arms. She released him to the floor where he took off, chasing after something she couldn't see.

Doug cast his eyes over her and down to the floor, where a sizable puddle of water had accumulated around her muddy feet.

"Did you bring any rain gear?"

She gestured to her windbreaker.

He raised a doubtful eyebrow and shrugged. "Come on. Let's get you settled." Grabbing an umbrella from a bucket by the door, he headed outside. She took one too, and, bracing herself, stepped back into the torrential rain and followed him to her car, which he examined with a skeptical look.

"Pretty much a miracle that you made it here in this thing."

"Fabulous," she snapped. "Just what I need. Another man taking potshots at my car."

He raised his eyebrows again, but said nothing.

She opened her trunk and pulled out one suitcase, letting him take the other. "Please get me out of this rain."

"Follow me."

She followed him up a low hill to the Laundry. The entire first floor was one big room filled with washing machines, dryers, and a type of machine she'd never seen before that had two large rollers in a wooden frame and a hand crank. "What are those things?"

"Mangles."

"Excuse me?"

"The cabin staff press the sheets and towels and tablecloths with them. There's the bathroom. I've been told there are six rooms upstairs with bunk beds. I don't think you have a room-mate, at this time. Men and boys aren't allowed upstairs except for very special occasions. 'No fraternizing.' They keep to long-standing traditions. It can feel a bit old-fashioned here."

"That's okay. I've always felt old-fashioned," she said. It was the truth.

"You know about the no cell phone rule?"

"Mrs. Hodges told me they were strongly discouraged."

"For guests, they're strongly discouraged, so people can take a true vacation, just like in the good old days. Staff are expected not to use their cell phones in front of the guests. It's all part of the vibe, but it's an easy rule to follow. The only place to get decent reception is in the main office."

"Really? Is there Wi-Fi in this building?"

He shook his head.

Well. That was going to be an adjustment for her parents, not being able to reach her by text whenever they wanted to. On the other hand, social media had pretty much been a nightmare for her for the past couple of years. The thought of really discon-necting from the rest of the world felt like a relief. She smiled at Doug and shrugged.

He smiled back. "So, I'm going to have to leave you at this point. Here's the lamp. Do you know how to put that out?"

"Yes. But you?"

"I'll be fine."

"Hi, Doug," came a singsong voice from upstairs. "I thought I was having a dream, but there actually is a man in here."

Doug tensed beside her. They arrived at the foot of the stairs. At the top stood a long-legged brunette wearing a skimpy teddy. It was freezing in this building and Heidi had every intention of wrapping herself in flannel PJs. She waved at the woman.

"Just dropping off our newest colleague. Janet, head waitress, meet Heidi, the new cook. Janet can show you your room."

"Yes. The special room." Her voice sounded syrupy but venomous at the same time. "For the special new colleague. She gets one all to herself. Only us small-time waitresses and cabin girls need to share."

"That's right, Janet," Doug said. "Make her feel welcome. You know just how."

Janet gave him the finger. Heidi wanted to intervene. She wanted no bad blood her first night, but there was obviously a history here. And though she had yet to say a word, Janet did not like her already.

Bitchy colleague, check.

"You're not allowed to be here, Doug."

"I'm leaving. Goodnight." He held the lantern to Heidi's face. Beneath his stern countenance, she detected a hint of wry sympathy. As she took the lantern from his hand, his warm fingers brushed her icy ones. He hesitated a moment before leaning forward. "Careful," he whispered. "There be dragons."

"Thanks for all your help," she called after him.

"Take off your jacket and shoes down there, if you don't mind," Janet said. "We try not to track in mud up here. Take your time. Who cares that it's the middle of the night and some of us need to get up to work tomorrow?"

"Sorry." Heidi toed off her sneakers and socks, and climbed the stairs barefoot, lugging her two suitcases. "I got lost on the way here, and the rain didn't help."

"Whatever," Janet said. "Follow me." Janet led her down the hall to the third door on the right. "The rooms are all the same. I made your bed, so it's ready for you to dive in. Any questions?"

"Are the sheets shorted?"

Janet laughed, despite herself. "I knew I forgot something."

RAINY DAYS

Every morning she made breakfast for the staff, which they ate in the room where she'd first met Doug, around an enormous wooden table. She usually served a big pan of scrambled eggs and piles of pancakes, or coffee cake and a soufflé if she was feeling especially creative. She was gratified by how appreciative the staff and the guests were of her culinary skills.

Her parents and, while he had been in the picture, Alan, had been unenthusiastic recipients of her cooking. They disliked anything that smacked of variety or surprise in any aspect of their daily lives. They disapproved of this newfound passion and all the time and money she had spent on the weekend culinary classes she insisted on pursuing in the years after college, when she had a perfectly serviceable degree in accounting.

With Alan moving up in his family's firm, you won't need to work anyway, in accounting or cooking. Our grandchildren will have a stay-at-home mom, just like you did. And Alan can make that possible. He wants a traditional family.

They didn't understand that she wanted to work, and that she was nowhere near ready to have children. Not that that was any concern right now, with Alan out of the picture.

"Hey, Spacy."

Heidi turned from the stovetop, surprised to find Doug standing there, plate in hand. It was her third day on the job and the first time they'd spoken since the night she arrived. "I'm sorry. Did you ask me something?"

"I said twice that the pancakes are delicious and asked twice if you were giving out seconds."

Heidi smiled, embarrassed, and slid three more large blueberry pancakes off the griddle and onto Doug's plate.

"Thanks. What planet were you on, anyway?" His gray-blue eyes seemed able to read her far too easily.

"Excuse me?"

He grinned at her. "Spacy."

"Don't call me Spacy," she said. "I don't like that nickname. Or any nickname."

"Then wake up," he said. "That was some intense conversation you were having in your head, I could tell. I thought you were about to start talking to yourself, or to whoever it was in your head you were talking to. All I'm saying is you're here now, Heidi. Be here."

She glared at him. "What are you, some kind of spiritual guru?"

He shrugged, offering an embarrassed grin that was pretty hard to resist. "That's just what I'm trying to tell myself, that's all." He backed out of the kitchen. "Thanks for breakfast. It's a big improvement over the runny eggs your predecessor dished out, believe me."

"You're welcome." She found she couldn't be angry at him, and smiled back, feeling warm inside.

Breakfast was the only time of the day that she usually saw Doug. He arrived at the table, smelling of pine and smoke and sweat, having already been up three hours lighting fires in all the cabins. In the old days, apparently, the goal was to have them all lit by six, so the pipes had time to heat and the guests could get warm water for their showers. While the resort had entered the modern era and now had hot water piped into the cabins, tradition still dictated that the fires must be lit before the guests emerged from their bedrooms each morning. Doug usually went upstairs right after eating to go back to sleep for a couple of hours, so she was glad he had finally made a point of speaking to her.

Because of the ceaseless rain, she spent her free time in her room, which she found Spartan but cozy. Old, durable patchwork quilts covered both upper and lower bunks. The remaining furniture consisted of a rod and several hooks on the walls to hang things, an old, heavy bureau, a wooden straightbacked chair by the window, and an oval-shaped, handmade rag rug of many different colors. She believed her room, with its sloping roof, was the smallest of the six rooms above the Laundry and hoped that meant she wouldn't be getting a roommate.

Not that she didn't occasionally wish for company, but it was hard to feel lonely when the names of numerous previous occupants were carved or inked into the wooden walls. Hardly any portion of the room remained untouched. Heidi spent some enjoyable hours studying these memorials from her predecessors. Many came in lists: "Callie, Emily, Inge, Jessica, Toni, Mary Ellen—Summer, 1981." Some were solo names with a brief message: "Sarah, Summer of 1993: I'll miss my Home in the Woods," or "Morgan, Summer 1976: Lost: something special. Found: memories for a lifetime." Her most exciting discovery was behind her headboard: "Summer, 1948 Cabin Staff— Dorothy, Ethel, Harriet, Mildred, Agnes, Josephine, Delores, Gertie." Those wonderful, old-fashioned names!

She couldn't find anything dating from earlier than that. She was tempted to study the walls of her colleagues' rooms when they were empty, but she could not in good conscience invade anyone's personal space. She certainly wanted them staying out of her room. Not that she had anything to hide. Well, nothing anyone would find out by searching her room, anyway. She sighed. It was time for her to get over that chapter of her life and move on.

The other staff treated her politely but didn't invite her to become part of the group they'd already established. Sometimes at night she'd hear giggling down the hall and know many of the cabin girls and waitresses were crammed into somebody's room, probably drinking and doing each other's toenails. She even heard male voices occasionally, despite the prohibition against "fraternizing." She didn't miss being part of it. She relished her solitude and her routine.

Okay, so she was a little lonely. She wouldn't mind having a friend, but most of the staff were still in college. Closest to her in age was Janet, but the two of them hadn't gotten off on the right foot. One waitress, Debbie, was a senior in college, here for the third summer, and although she was younger, she seemed quite mature for her age. Heidi would have liked to get to know her better, but Debbie spent all her free time helping Mrs. Hodges in the office.

There was also one cute and friendly waiter, Chris, who roomed above the kitchen near Doug. Monster also gifted Chris with animal remains on many mornings, though not as often as Doug, Chris said, because Monster liked Doug better. This was absolutely fine with Chris. Chris was attractive and fun, with warm brown eyes and copper curls falling over his forehead. An avid runner, he changed into running gear and headed down the long dirt road after the morning shift every day despite the incessant rain, perfectly happy to dodge puddles and raindrops for five miles.

Heidi found his energy appealing—who wouldn't? Of

course, as a senior in college, he was far too young for her to be interested in romantically, but she didn't mind that Chris included her in his flirtations, along with the rest of the female staff. It had been a long time since anyone had made her feel attractive. She thought of Doug, standing by her stove, holding out his plate for more pancakes, calling her Spacy, smiling at her. Two men were making her feel attractive. Not a bad feeling.

Each day, Heidi concluded her breakfast shift with a delivery to Pleasant Cottage, currently occupied by Miss Bertha Strickland, who had spent the same two weeks of every summer there for the past seventy years. Ninety now, Miss Strickland no longer made it to the main dining hall for breakfast or lunch, venturing out only for the evening meal. So, Heidi packed an old-fashioned picnic basket with a simple breakfast of warm muffins, a banana, and large Thermos of coffee, and for lunch, a ham and cheese sandwich on rye, and delivered the food to her cabin.

Heidi enjoyed this task. It was about an eight-minute walk from the main lodge to Pleasant Cottage, along a winding path covered with pine needles and bordered by large wet ferns. Through white pine and birch trees, she could see the dark, rain-pelted lake, and smell the cool, crisp freshness of damp vegetation. The cottage was one of several that offered a narrow path leading to a small private dock and lake access.

As usual, Heidi found the old woman wearing purple corduroys, dependable Clarks shoes (just like her grandmother had worn) and an elaborately hand-knit sweater, sitting in a rocker by a roaring fire, reading a large print mystery. On the screened-in porch, Heidi slipped out of the poncho and rain boots Mrs. Hodges had lent her and entered the cottage in stocking feet. She placed the picnic basket on the table.

"Do you know who did it yet?" She gestured to the hardcover in Miss Strickland's lap.

"Well, I thought it was surely the butler this time, but he's

just been found decapitated in the woodshed. So, no, not yet."
The old woman grinned. "Thank you, Heidi. You make a superb
ham and cheese sandwich and are a far more delightful person
than your predecessor. Now, go get your quiet time before your
next shift. I know how hard you girls work."

"Shall I put another log on the fire?" Heidi asked. "It'll be
chilly all day."

"No need, dear. Douglas will be by soon enough. He keeps
my fire going."

"Douglas?"

"Yes. Surely, you've met Douglas. The fire boy?" She peered
at Heidi over her maroon reading glasses.

"Well, yes, but we're on different schedules. Do you see him
often?"

"Oh, yes. I always get to know the fire boys. They're often the
most interesting of the employees. Well, last year's wasn't, but he
was an exception. This one is a bit older than they usually are
and very well read. He loves Shakespeare almost as much as I
do. He's read most of the plays. I challenged him to keep going.
I've never met anyone besides myself who's read them all."

"Really?" Heidi couldn't hide her surprise. "He hasn't even
been to college."

"No. Then again, neither have I," said Miss Strickland. "My
brother went to college. There was only money enough for one
of us. But the library was free. Thank you for my provisions,
dear. I'm eager to continue now." She raised her book slightly.

"Have a good day, Miss Strickland." Heidi backed away to the
door.

"Oh, I intend to." The old woman turned her attention once
again to her book.

3

AFTER HOURS

About ten days after she arrived, Chris pulled her aside in the kitchen after dinner, laying a friendly arm over her shoulder.

"It's Doug's day off tomorrow," he said quietly in her ear, "so he's actually agreed to hang out for a change, since he doesn't have to get up in the middle of the night. We got some beer. Will you join us?"

"Where?" she asked, surprised by how pleased she felt to be included, given that she was older than almost all the summer employees. It had continued to be rainy the whole time she'd been here, so she knew outdoors was not an option. "In the staff room?"

"Nah, we spend too much time around that table. In the lodge's living room."

"But that's off limits for staff."

Chris grinned. "So it is, which means we can't turn on any lights. And we have to be very quiet. And clean up after ourselves, of course. But it's by far the most comfortable space available for a larger group. And, as I mentioned before, we have beer. Janet and Debbie did a little road trip earlier today."

"Um." Heidi pressed her lips together. She was a rule-follower, generally, and didn't relish the thought of getting in trouble with Mrs. Hodges.

"Oh, come on, Heidi, live a little!" Chris said. "Doug's not going to stay if you're not there and I really don't want to be the only person here who knows how great he is. Since he tends to go for the mysterious silent man mystique, you know."

Heidi laughed. "Yes, he does do that." She hesitated. "But why should it make any difference if I'm there?"

Chris shrugged and winked at her. "What can I say? Apparently, it does. Come on, what's the worst that's going to happen? They're not going to fire the cook."

"I'm here because they already fired a cook this summer."

"Yeah, okay, but she couldn't cook. You can. Come on, please. Hang out with us. We'll have fun."

So, after the dining room tables had been set for the next morning, and the kitchen made spotless, and Mrs. Hodges had finished whatever business she had in the staff dining room and returned to her cabin, Heidi found herself tiptoeing into the lodge's living room with the rest of the giggling staff. They left on the staff dining room lights, which gave them just enough visibility to see each other in the room's shadows.

An enormous stag's head with massive antlers loomed over the fireplace, in front of which lay a thick bearskin rug, onto which sprawled two cabin girls who lived in nearby camps on the lake. Sofas and armchairs formed a semi-circle in front of the cold fireplace. Heidi sat in an armchair, slipped off her shoes and tucked her feet under her, noting that Doug had yet to make an appearance. Janet surprised her by handing her a beer. Debbie and two other waitstaff lounged on couches. A moment later, Harry and Ben, two of Mrs. Hodges' grandsons, appeared in the doorway, each carrying a twelve-pack. Harry was a recent college grad and Ben was still in college.

"Awesome!" Debbie jumped up, put her arms around Ben's waist, and gave him a kiss on the lips. "Will your grandmother be angry if she catches you 'fraternizing' with us again?" she teased.

"Furious. She might fire me." Ben opened a beer, pulled Debbie down onto the couch beside him, and planted a kiss on her temple.

Interesting. Apparently, there was romance in the air. Heidi glanced around the room to see if there were any others paired up, but Ben and Debbie seemed to be the only ones.

"I hope she fires me," Harry said, taking a seat on the floor and leaning against the couch. "I've been working here every damn summer since I was ten years old. I beg her to fire me all the time, but it doesn't do any good."

Heidi studied Harry, who wore thick dark glasses that made him look a bit like Clark Kent. She was pretty sure he was lying about wanting to get fired. He spent most of his time in the wood shop repairing broken furniture or making new furniture, and he seemed pretty content to her.

"I wish we could have a fire!" Ellie, one of the cabin girls, said. "It's so chilly in here."

Chris pulled the tab off a beer can and handed it to her. "This will warm you up, Ellie. Your limit is two."

"Oh, come on," she grumbled. "I'm not a baby. I'm seventeen."

"Yeah, underage, so you're lucky to be hanging out with us mature adults," Chris said. "And I'm not cleaning up your barf again. Two. Everyone got that? Ellie's limit is two beers tonight."

Ellie burst into giggles, delighted with this attention from Chris.

"Did you get a head start on us?" He gave her a sharp glance, though it was obvious he was just pretending to be stern.

She shook her head and giggled some more. Heidi smiled.

How sweet to be seventeen and have a slightly older and really cute guy flirting with you in such a caring way.

Footsteps sounded on the back stairs. A moment later, Doug entered from the staff dining room. He wore faded jeans, scuffed loafers, and a plaid flannel shirt over a tee shirt. His messy brown hair fell nearly to his eyes and his beard was scruffy. The energy in the room became charged the moment he appeared. He was very attractive, in his quiet, rugged way, and she wasn't the only one who thought so.

Heidi hugged her knees. She'd never done this before, hung out in a group with a bunch of cute, fun guys drinking beer. She'd always been Alan's devoted girlfriend, and he generally kept her to himself. All through college and in the years afterward, she hadn't even realized how much she wanted something different from their staid routines. She turned, feeling Doug's gaze on her, sensed him scolding her for her ruminating thoughts. In her head, she heard his voice: *Wake up.* She smiled at him, and he smiled back, his eyes crinkling.

"The man himself." Chris handed Doug a beer.

"Thanks." Doug pulled open the tab.

"The old guy gets to sleep in tomorrow, folks," Chris said, "so let's make sure he stays up all night."

Doug shrugged. "I'm fine with that, but as I'm the only one who gets to sleep in tomorrow, I'd advise against it." He glanced at Heidi, his smile almost shy, and settled into the armchair beside her.

"Please can we play a game?" Ellie cried. "I never got to play *Never Have I Ever* with you guys!"

"Because you were puking your guts out," Chris said. "I didn't get to play either, since I was holding your head over the toilet."

"So, don't you want to play now?" she asked, winningly.

"Sure," he said. "I'm game."

"Okay," said Janet. "Everyone have a beverage?" She looked around the room. "Everyone in?"

"How do you play?" Heidi asked. Every face in the room turned to stare at her.

"Are you serious?" Ben said. "Have you been hiding under a rock your whole life?"

Heidi's cheeks heated, making her grateful for the dim light. "I guess so."

"What drinking games do you know?" Debbie asked.

Memories of watching Alan play beer pong at college on a couple of rare occasions flashed through her mind. Other than that, she didn't know any drinking games. "It wasn't really my thing," she admitted.

"It's easy," Ellie said, practically bouncing on the bear rug. "We go around the room and everyone takes a turn saying, 'Never have I ever... kissed a boy,' for example, and if you have kissed a boy, you have to drink."

"Okay," Heidi said. "I think I can handle that."

"I'm going to sit this one out," Doug said.

"Don't be that way, Doug!" Ellie cried. "You never hang out with us. Come on. Be fun for once in your life. Pleeeaaase?"

Doug shook his head, smiling. "Fine. I'll play."

"Great," Ellie said. "You start."

Doug looked contemplative for a moment, then said, "Never have I ever gone skinny dipping in this lake."

Everyone in the room besides Doug, Heidi, and Chris drank.

"No way!" Chris said incredulously. "How did I miss this?"

"We haven't gone yet this summer," Harry said. "First full moon. Your turn, Heidi."

"Okay." She thought for a moment. "Never have I ever been mistaken for being older than I actually am."

Everyone in the room laughed. Doug, Janet, and the cabin girls drank.

"I don't even get carded in bars most of the time," Ellie said, smugly. "So, I must look twenty-one."

"Sorry to break it to you, Ellie, but that's not why you don't get carded," Ben said.

Heidi sipped her beer to hide her surprise. It would never have occurred to her to try to get into a bar before she reached the legal drinking age, not that she spent much time in bars after that, either. Nor would she have thought that bartenders might not card a girl just because she was pretty, which is what she assumed Ben was implying about Ellie.

"Heidi, I bet you're still going to get carded when you're forty," Debbie said. "You'll be happy about it then."

Heidi observed the easy manner in which Debbie and Ben cuddled with each other, the way he wrapped his arm around her shoulder, the way she twined her warm brown fingers through his paler, sun-kissed ones. What was this uncomfortable feeling inside her? Envy? She turned her head to find Doug watching her. He lowered his gaze, then looked up at her again and winked. She turned away, heart racing, and pressed her lips together so she wouldn't smile like a total goofball and let her little crush on Doug become blatantly obvious to the rest of the room.

"My turn. Never have I ever swallowed a live goldfish," Harry said.

Ben drank to the groans of everyone else in the room. "Hey, don't knock it till you've tried it. That little fish was de-lish." He grinned when the cabin girls squealed in disgust. When it was his turn, he said, "Never have I ever dropped my bathing suit in poison ivy and had a seriously itchy crotch for half the summer."

Harry shook his head and drank. Heidi found herself laughing and heard Doug's warm laugh beside her. She cast another glance his way, and he caught her gaze and held it, his eyes alight. She felt warm inside, liking everyone in the room, even Janet. Until it was Janet's turn.

"Never have I ever been in prison," she said, looking straight at Doug.

Heidi glanced at Doug in surprise. He stared back at Janet, his expression morphing from friendly to stony. Everyone grew quiet and stared at him. Several people gasped.

"Well played, Janet," Harry said quietly. "What the hell's the matter with you? I don't remember you being such a bitch last summer."

"I think the staff has the right to know who they're working with. And if I were a guest in this place, I sure would want to know if the guy coming into my cabin every morning when I'm asleep was an ex-con."

"If any guests find out, your ass is history." Ben's tone was quiet and threatening. "Chill out, everyone. We've known Doug for years. He came up here with his family every summer till... anyway, we vouch for him. Seriously, Janet. What is your problem? I can't believe you're the same girl we knew last summer. Is this about Chad?"

Janet looked slightly abashed, but still angry. "Chad was counting on being fire boy again and he didn't find out till May that she'd given the job to someone else."

"Chad should have known at the end of last summer he wasn't ever going to be fire boy again," Harry said. "He had the work ethic of a sloth. If Doug weren't here, I'd be fire boy for the umpteenth time, not Chad, so believe me, I'm glad Doug's here. Now I only have to get up at 3:30 in the morning once a week."

The fact that Harry and Ben were not surprised or particularly concerned by Janet's revelation did lessen the alarm in the room, but most of the staff were still looking at Doug uneasily. Heidi kept her gaze averted. She was astonished. What in the world had he done that had landed him in prison? How long had he been there? Had he just gotten out?

Then, to her horror, she remembered the comment she'd made to him the night she arrived, when they were still standing in the dark, about being sure he hadn't escaped from a maximum-security prison. She remembered how he'd frozen at her words, how she'd felt the anger vibrating off him. She clapped a hand over her mouth and stared at him, aghast.

He caught her gaze and then lowered his eyes in disappointment and possibly shame. Oh, no! She hadn't been thinking what he thought she was thinking. She was surprised, no question, and a little uneasy, but it was the memory of her poorly timed joke that distressed her most at the moment, not the surprising revelation about him.

"What did you do?" Ellie blurted out the question on everyone's mind.

Doug stood up, his knees cracking. "This isn't something I want to talk about. I'm heading to bed. Good night, everyone."

With that, he left the room. They listened to his footsteps on the stairs and overhead, walking down the hallway, and then the sound of a door opening and shutting. They remained silent and still for a few long moments. Then, one by one, they stood, gathered up their beer cans and prepared to depart.

"I just thought people should know," Janet said defensively.

Harry shrugged. "Well. Now, they know. 'Night, Janet."

4

BREAKFAST IN BED

The next morning, the staff sat around the table in a somber mood. When Mrs. Hodges came in to speak to Heidi about the dinner menu, she took in all their gloomy faces and asked, "Did someone die?"

They looked at each other guiltily. Doug made no appearance all morning. None of them looked like they had slept well, and Janet's eyes were red from weeping. Heidi had heard muffled sobs through the wall and wondered who was crying. She was surprised to see it had been Janet, though she had limited sympathy, as Janet had brought all that negative attention on herself. She sensed no one approved of her revealing Doug's secret that way.

"We're just tired of all this rain," Debbie said. "Will the sun ever come out again?"

"It always has," Mrs. Hodges said. This reminded Heidi of Doug, who had given her the same response on her first night here, when she asked if the power would ever come back on. She suspected he felt ashamed and exposed and wondered if he would speak to her again. She wondered if she should even want him to.

All night her parents' warnings had drummed through her head, their insistence that she was naïve and vulnerable and ripe for being taken advantage of. To a point, she agreed with them. That's exactly what made her such easy prey for Alan, though her parents had for years perceived him as a protector, not a control freak. Their perspective had changed when they realized how unhappy she'd been in the relationship but, if anything, it made them even more fearful on her behalf.

Her shock at learning that Doug had spent time in prison was made worse by her newfound awareness that she was very attracted to him. He was the first man in a long time that she'd caught herself daydreaming about. Ridiculous as it was, those fantasies zoomed right past the parts where they kissed and fell in love and involved introducing her parents to this handsome, rugged guy who embraced both hard physical labor and serious intellectual pursuits.

She was already worrying about what they would think about him just starting college at the age of twenty-six, and the possibility that he might want to major in English, given his apparent interest in Shakespeare. Her parents considered the whole concept of majoring in English, and the liberal arts in general, to be frivolous and irresponsible, unless one's life ambition was to be an English teacher. As they paid for her college, they had expected to approve of her course of study, and she hadn't even questioned their right to do that. When they said they didn't consider an elective in Victorian novels worth however many thousands of dollars they calculated it to be, she'd been disappointed, but hadn't challenged them.

She didn't have to imagine what their response would be to their learning that Doug was getting a late start at college because he'd been incarcerated. What had he done? she wondered. Maybe she had proven herself a poor judge of character in the past, but she liked him. It couldn't have been that bad, whatever it was. Ben and Harry didn't seem to think so, at any rate. But her parents would never, ever give their approval to her being romantically involved with an ex-convict, that much she knew for certain.

On the other hand, she was twenty-seven years old. She didn't need their approval. Did she? Was it pathetic that she still wanted it so much?

Probably.

Definitely. At the very least, she didn't want to hurt them again. They had been so devastated when everything with Alan exploded. But if she hadn't been so accommodating and compliant with everyone else's wishes in the first place, if she'd insisted instead on what she wanted....

Looking up, she saw Debbie waiting impatiently by the stove for her next order.

She sighed. *Wake up, Heidi.*

By the time the breakfast shift was over, there had still been no sign of Doug. He always ate an enormous breakfast. She knew he must be hungry. So, she prepared a tray for him, with plates of eggs, toast, bacon, pancakes, coffee, and orange juice.

"Will you take this up for him?" she asked Chris.

"I'll carry it up the stairs," he said. "But I think it would mean more if he knew it was coming from you."

"No females are allowed on the second floor of this building."

Chris rolled his eyes. "All right, Heidi? You seriously need to chill. Have you always been such a good little girl?"

Heidi sighed. "I know, I know. You're right. And no, not always." She cringed, briefly imagining what Chris would think of her if he ever found out what she'd done. "And don't speak to me that way, either. It's obnoxious."

He smiled approvingly, as if pleased to see her be just a little assertive.

She sighed. "Chris, did you know? About Doug?"

Chris shook his head. "I didn't have a clue. Not sure I want to know any more details, either." He picked up the tray and led the way. For the first time, Heidi climbed the stairs to the second floor. She followed Chris down a long, narrow hallway, walking over a faded, practically threadbare Oriental carpet. Frames with old, yellowed photographs of the resort in generations past hung on the walls.

Chris stopped outside a door. A light shone underneath, indicating that Doug was awake. Heidi knocked. There was no answer. She knocked again.

"Who is it?" Doug said gruffly.

"Room service," Chris said. "You decent?"

"Yes."

Chris nodded, and Heidi pushed open the door. The room was significantly larger than her little space over the Laundry. Wide windows with no curtains let in gray daylight. Rain pelted the glass. Doug lay on a double bed, half under the covers and propped up on pillows, wearing glasses that gave him a surprisingly professorial look. The lamp on the bedside table was on, and he held a book in his hand. Monster sprawled on Doug's stomach, his long black tail twitching ominously, his emerald eyes observing them with a watchful gaze.

"We brought you breakfast," Heidi said.

Doug looked back and forth between her and Chris, obviously surprised. He cleared his throat. "Thank you."

"Sorry about last night, dude," Chris said. "We're not going to pry, but we're here for you, if you want to talk."

"Thanks," Doug said, stiffly. "I'm fine." He pushed himself to sit upright, eliciting an extended, angry meow from Monster. The moment he stopped moving, Monster resettled himself, this time on Doug's lap. Doug placed his book, *Tess of the d'Urbervilles,* on the patchwork quilt with the pages face downward so as not to lose his place.

"I hear that's hilarious," Chris said, nodding at the book.

Doug shrugged. "Your typical summer beach read."

"You read a lot," Heidi said.

Doug looked at her, surprised. "Yes. How did you know?"

She flushed. "Miss Strickland mentioned that you both liked Shakespeare."

He nodded, eyeing her curiously. Chris cast a mischievous glance her way. Okay, so she was talking to a guest about Doug. There was no reason to read anything into that.

"She brought it up," Heidi said, defensively. "I wasn't asking questions about you or anything."

"I didn't think you were," Doug said. "Sorry, this cat has me very well trained. I don't dare move again and risk his displeasure. Heidi, would you bring that little table over so Chris can put down the tray?"

She did. Chris set down the tray and, with a dramatic gesture, pulled the rounded aluminum plate covers off the two plates, revealing the substantial breakfast Heidi had prepared.

Doug nodded, impressed. "That's really sweet of you two. Thank you."

"It's all Heidi," Chris said. "I just carried it up the stairs. Okay, sorry to dash, but I've got to get my run in before the lunch shift."

"You're crazy," Heidi said. "It's pouring out there."

"You want to see crazy, hang around me some day when I don't get my run in," Chris said. "Later, guys." He left the room, shutting the door behind him.

Heidi and Doug stared at each other.

"I should be going, too." She headed to the door.

"Thanks for breakfast," he said quietly.

She paused, her hand on the doorknob, then turned to face

him again. "Last night, I think you misinterpreted my expression."

Doug shrugged. "I interpreted your expression as horror. Was that a misinterpretation? It's okay, Heidi. I don't blame you."

"Well, I *was* horrified, but at myself. My first night here, I thought you were so hypersensitive and prickly. Even in the dark, I could tell you had a strong, negative reaction when I made that silly comment about you not being a serial killer escaped from a maximum-security prison. And last night, after I realized you had been in prison, I understood why that joke upset you. That's what I was horrified about: that I was tactless without meaning to be. I was upset about me. Not about you."

He studied her, contemplating her words. After a moment, he nodded. "Okay."

"I mean, you're not a serial killer, are you?"

He shook his head. "I am not."

"I don't want to pry."

"I appreciate that."

She waited for him to say more, but he clearly did not intend to.

"Okay," she said, turning away. "See you later."

"Heidi," Doug said.

She held onto the doorknob, waiting.

"You don't need to be afraid of me."

She let out a breath of air she hadn't even known she'd been holding in. "That's a relief." She smiled. "I'm assuming that's your way of telling me you haven't killed anybody."

His face paled. He swallowed, his lips clamped shut. She stared at him, knowing that an expression of horror returned to her face.

"Oh," she whispered. She bit her lip and opened the door. "See you, Doug."

5

SUNSHINE, AT LAST

At long last, out came the sun. Wednesday of the following week, they were able to take the guests on an outing. It was all-hands-on-deck. Canoes, rowboats, and kayaks lined the small beach area on the far side of the cabins, while a party barge waited at the dock for equipment and folks preferring to avoid exercise. The staff loaded coolers, barbecue grills, pancake griddles, all kinds of cooking utensils, the biggest cast iron frying pan Heidi had ever seen in her life, and badminton equipment onto the party barge for transportation to an island in the middle of White Pine Lake.

Doug was there too, of course. Though they had been polite with each other, they had exchanged few words during the past week. Since her first foray into socializing with the staff had ended on such an unpleasant note, she had drawn back into her own shell and talked very little with anyone beyond what she had to for work.

She repeatedly rehashed the last conversation she'd had with Doug, to see if there might be any other way to interpret his words—or rather, his silence. Had he actually killed someone?

Because if he had been imprisoned for murder, Heidi didn't think she wanted to get to know him any better. She was not the kind of woman who got turned on by that kind of thing, like all those crazy women who wanted to marry men who'd been convicted of gruesome crimes.

But if it had been murder, then why would he be out so soon? Maybe he'd gone to prison as a juvenile? Surely if Mrs. Hodges considered him dangerous, she would not have hired him, or at the very least, not given him a job that required him to go into the cabins of sleeping guests. And Doug had flat out denied that he was a serial killer and volunteered that she didn't need to be afraid of him. She could just hear her parents: *What would you expect a serial killer to say, Heidi?*

Doug also didn't seem to be talking much to anyone these days. Today, he wore a gray tee shirt and blue jean shorts. She couldn't help but admire the muscles in his arms and thighs. Working muscles, she thought. Alan had gym bunny muscles, his sculpted look the product of considerable time and effort and self-examination in the mirror. Doug chopped and carried wood. He didn't need to spend time in a gym.

Oh, she didn't want to think any more about men! How magnificent the dark lake looked and smelled—such cleansing, pine-scented freshness! And blue sky, for the fourth day in a row. She couldn't keep from smiling.

She ended up canoeing with Janet, who sat helmsman.

"Try not to splash me," Janet said. "I want to keep my hair dry." She had been up early curling it and Heidi had to admit it looked pretty, falling in gentle brown waves around her face, though why she had put the effort in on a day when they'd all be working outside, Heidi had no idea.

They paddled in silence most of the way.

"So, what's your story?" Janet asked as they neared the island. "Any reason you keep to yourself so much?"

"Just an introvert," Heidi said. "Nothing exciting about me." The skin on the back of her neck prickled.

"You don't like people?"

"I like people, Janet."

"But you prefer your own company?"

Heidi tensed, her temper rising. She braced for Janet to goad her again.

"I Googled you," Janet said.

Heidi closed her eyes and cringed. But really, how much could Janet have found out, not having any acquaintances in common? "I've been enjoying taking a break from the Internet," she said, keeping her voice neutral. "I'm surprised how happy I've been not to have access to Wi-Fi."

"Me too," Janet admitted. "But I was covering the office yesterday and got bored. You look really pretty in your engagement picture."

Oh. That. She'd forgotten about having their engagement photo in their local paper. Since when did their town's little paper go online?

"Cute guy, too," Janet continued. "I don't see any wedding ring now, though. You don't act like you're engaged or married. What happened? Did he leave you at the altar?"

Heidi gritted her teeth. What a bitch. It was one thing to do the Internet research and quite another to be so catty about what she'd learned. "Have you ever thought about minding your own business?"

"Come on," Janet said. "Spill the beans. What happened?"

Heidi said nothing. She really didn't want to talk about it. What she wanted to do was make a voodoo doll of whoever invented the Internet and stick pins in it. Google sucked. Social media sucked. Engagement photos sucked. Bitchy colleagues sucked. She glanced behind her.

Janet eyed her curiously. "What did you do? Lie to him?

Sleep with his best friend? Why did your fiancé dump you? Or are you the one who dumped him?"

The island loomed before them, easy swimming distance.

"You know what?" Heidi said, sliding her paddle onto the floor of the boat. "I think I'm going to take a dip." She stood up suddenly. The canoe rocked beneath her.

"Sit down, you idiot!" Janet yelled. "Do you want to tip us over?"

Heidi made a quick glance around the boat to confirm they weren't carrying anything of value. "I'm going to dive in, Janet. I'll just be a minute." She stood on her seat, balancing precariously, and sidled to the left. The canoe rocked some more.

"Heidi! Sit down." Janet's face was red with rage, as if sensing what Heidi intended to do. "My hair!"

Heidi dived into the water, feeling the canoe tipping as she went. She emerged to find Janet spluttering in the water beside her, hair plastered all over her face, the canoe upside down and the paddles floating away.

"You bitch!" Janet screamed when she came up for air. "You did that on purpose."

"It was a complete accident, I swear," Heidi said drily. "I've got one paddle—can you get the other?"

"No, it's your fault. You can get it."

"Come on, Janet, help me tip her back over."

"You did it on purpose. Tip it over yourself!"

Janet started swimming to the island with a steady crawl, dragging her life preserver behind her. Heidi stared after her, treading water, admiring the fact that Janet was a strong swimmer and wondering what in the world she was going to do now. Guests in the nearby canoes and kayaks looked at Heidi somewhat helplessly. Then she saw Doug on the shore, taking off his shoes and shirt, wading in and swimming in her direction. She treaded water, waiting for him.

"Hi," he said, when he reached her, water dripping off his beard, which she noticed he had trimmed.

"Hi," she said. "Thanks for coming to help. Sorry about this."

"She must have really pissed you off." He grinned. She liked the way his gray-blue eyes lit up when he smiled. And those really were some impressive muscles, now that she could see him up close and without his shirt on. Her cheeks heated, and she ducked her head underwater, pretending to evade an invisible horsefly.

He swam under the canoe and, in a minute, had it right side up again. He put the paddle in. Heidi swam after the other paddle and slipped it into the canoe with its mate, along with her life jacket, which was too cumbersome to swim any distance in.

The canoe blocked their view of the island, which also meant that no one on the island could see them. They treaded water for a moment, looking at each other in silence. She had a strong urge to close the short distance between them and kiss him. But she had never been the type of woman to do something spontaneous like that, even though she very much wanted to, and he was looking at her in a way that made her think he wouldn't mind.

Don't be stupid, Heidi, a little voice warned her. *The only thing you know about this man is that he's been in prison. And that he might have killed someone.*

You sure never had this kind of stirred up feeling about Alan, another voice said.

Doug cleared his throat. "You want to get back in or just swim it to shore?"

"Swimming to shore is fine," she said.

He grabbed the rope and tugged the canoe behind him as he swam a powerful breaststroke, his head dipping in and out of the water.

When they arrived at the island, Doug beached the canoe. A group of kids were throwing horseshoes under Harry's supervision. One badminton net was set up and already had a rousing game going. Chris and Ben were in the process of setting up the other net. The shrieks and laughter of the guests made her smile. Her family had never taken this kind of vacation, but if they had, she would have loved it.

"You, uh, want to borrow my shirt?" Doug asked. He stood in front of her, blocking her view of guests and staff alike. "It's dry."

Heidi glanced down and gasped in alarm. Her white tee shirt had gone completely see-through, revealing not only the outline of her bra, but a visual of her breasts as well, that left nothing to the imagination. Not quite the professional look she'd been going for. Heat flooded her face. She crossed her arms, covering her chest.

"Hey. It's all right." He leapt away and was back a moment later, handing her his gray tee shirt.

She put it on, and since the shirt was so big on her, she managed to wriggle out of her white one, which she laid on a rock to dry. "Thanks," she said, aware of her soaking shorts and wishing she'd thought to wear a bathing suit. "But what about you?"

He shrugged. "I was planning on working on my tan today."

"Bullshit," she said.

He grinned. "I'm okay. You better get all your kitchen staff to pitch in chopping the onions and potatoes. It takes forever."

Thirty-five guests and twelve staff. They needed to slice enough onions and potatoes for forty-seven people. The knives for the job were none too sharp, and the aluminum plates that served as cutting boards made a screechy sound each time a knife sliced through a potato or onion. Heidi hadn't thought to check their outdoor cooking equipment ahead of time, which was a rookie mistake on her part. She was going to have to do something about those knives before the next outing. Emptying her plate into the enormous frying pan, she grabbed another onion, tears streaming down her cheeks. Beside her, Ellie and the other cabin girls were also weeping. Other staff diced potatoes, looking sympathetically at the onion choppers, but not offering to trade tasks.

"Why does this happen?" Ellie whimpered, wiping her face with the back of her hand.

"Onions have sulfur and an enzyme called synthase, and when you cut into them, they react and produce a gas that irritates the glands that make us cry," Heidi said. Her colleagues looked at her in surprise. "One of my cooking teachers made us memorize that. I don't know why."

"Well, I'm not going to remember it," Ellie muttered.

"Show off," said Janet, who had taken off her own wet shirt to reveal a flattering pink bikini top.

Heidi sighed and wiped her eyes with the back of her hand. She was not going to give Janet the pleasure of reacting to her anymore today. Glancing up, she found Doug watching her from the other side of the fire he was tending. He was in charge of grilling the steaks along with Mark Hodges, a wiry man with a thick graying beard who was Wanda Hodges' son and Ben's father. She smiled and lowered her head.

An hour later, the enticing aroma of sautéed onions and potatoes filled the air, mingling with the almost intoxicating smell of steaks grilled on an open fire. Chris and Janet hoisted the large orange thermoses of lemonade, iced tea, and coffee onto one of the picnic tables. The guests formed a line, aluminum plates in hand.

"Steaks ready?" she asked Mark, squatting beside him. "They smell to die for."

"Ready. You know what to say?"

"Excuse me?" she asked.

"Cook has to say, 'Dinner is prepared!'"

"Really?" She glanced at Doug for confirmation.

He nodded. "Tradition."

"You can trust this guy to tell you the truth. He'd give you the shirt off his back," Mark said, deadpan.

Heidi laughed, glancing at Doug again. Well, she knew that was true, and it was a very comfortable shirt too, so big on her she was practically swimming in it.

"All right, then." She stood up, ladle in hand, assuming her position by the fried potatoes and onions. "Hey, everyone!"

The crowd silenced instantly.

"Dinner is prepared!" she shouted.

The guests burst into raucous clapping and cheering.

"Is this response tradition too?" she asked Doug.

"Oh, yeah." He kept his eyes on the steaks, but he was smiling.

Back in the kitchen, fatigued from being out in the sun for the first time in weeks, the staff unpacked baskets and washed equipment, working in silence under time pressure to be ready to serve dinner. How the guests were going to eat another bite after the lunch they'd devoured, followed by pancakes and maple syrup for dessert, Heidi had no idea. She had a light supper planned, mostly salads and quiche. They all stopped what they were doing when Mrs. Hodges entered the kitchen, a rare occurrence.

"Squabbling among the staff in front of our guests is impermissible," she said, the expression on her wrinkled yet handsome face stern and formidable. "Would someone please tell me what the hell happened this afternoon?"

For a moment, Heidi felt nothing but surprise and confusion as she tried to imagine what had upset Mrs. Hodges so much. From her perspective, it had been a most agreeable day. Then she noticed the rest of the staff surreptitiously glancing at her and Janet, and she cringed, remembering the canoe incident. She dropped her eyes, embarrassed. She didn't want to have to explain that.

After a moment of awkward silence, Janet stepped forward. "I'm sorry, Mrs. Hodges. I was trying to make friendly conversation by telling Heidi how pretty she looked in her engagement picture last year."

Heidi looked up, horrified. She stared, silently pleading with Janet not to say any more, but she continued:

"She's not wearing a ring now, so I don't know if she's engaged, or married, or if the whole thing got called off for some reason. I just asked her what happened, that's all. Not my business, I know, but if she didn't want to talk about it, she should have just said so, instead of tipping the canoe over. That seems like a bit of an overreaction to me. I mean, obviously I know now that it's a sensitive subject, so I'll leave it alone."

Right. Heidi gritted her teeth. Now that you've excited everyone else's curiosity, you'll leave it alone. Heat started at Heidi's chest and crawled up her neck to her face to her scalp. She was blushing, one of her horrible, want to crawl under a table and hide kind of blushes, in front of the entire staff. Doug, Chris, Debbie, Ellie, all the staff: they were all there in the kitchen, all looking at her and then turning their eyes away. They all now knew that she had been engaged, and no longer was, and that something terribly embarrassing had happened that she really didn't want to talk about. Now the rumor mill was going to start flying, just like it had in her hometown. It seemed like she wasn't ever going to be able to get away from this. Her one terrible lapse in judgment was probably going to haunt her for the rest of her life.

"Well," Mrs. Hodges said, after a moment. "Tipping the canoe seems like a perfectly appropriate response to me. Janet, come see me in my office once everything here is cleaned up." With that, Mrs. Hodges left the room.

Heidi's cheeks continued to burn. Her eyes watered. She turned to her sink, wanting to hide from all these curious eyes, begging her blush to go away, begging her eyes not to cry. She resumed scrubbing a cast iron griddle, more furious with herself than with Janet. Janet was being a busybody, but it was her own strong reactions: tipping the canoe, blushing like a tomato, that signaled to everyone else that she had done something she would much prefer to hide.

A few minutes later, out of the corner of her eye, she saw Janet lurking beside her. She couldn't believe the woman wanted to speak to her again. She refused to acknowledge her and kept right on scrubbing.

"Well, Heidi," Janet said, her voice low. "I'm sure you'll be thrilled if you managed to get me fired. Thanks a million."

Heidi scrubbed harder, eyes down. "Oh, please," she said, through gritted teeth, "You're not going to get fired. And if you do get fired, it won't be my fault. I can't help it if you insist on being a bitch. Just do me a favor and leave me alone."

"No problem," Janet snapped back. "But you might want to locate some Wi-Fi and Google your new boyfriend. You can find out everything he did online." Janet paused, and then in a tone unexpectedly void of hostility, she added, "Seriously, do your research. I know he's cute, but he's got a serious temper. Do yourself a favor and find out the details before you get in too deep."

When she was sure Janet had gone, Heidi scanned the room

for Doug. He was unloading another pack of aluminum dishes onto the counter. She found his somber eyes, which made clear that he had overheard Janet talking about him. He nodded curtly on his way out of the kitchen, leaving Heidi to wonder what kind of *serious temper* lands someone in prison.

6

MOON AND STARS ABOVE

Heidi loved a spotless kitchen. Something about shiny counters, empty dishwashers, cupboards full of clean, neatly stacked dishes, an immaculate stovetop, and a refrigerator stocked with all the ingredients she needed for the next day washed away the stress of a chaotic dinner hour. She managed to be the last one to leave every night. She had been there less than three weeks and she already felt territorial over this kitchen. The industrial dishwasher predated the one at Angie's, where she'd worked this past year, and it cleaned dishes better. She took off her hairnet, wiped her hands dry on a dish towel, and surveyed the cleanliness with satisfaction.

Now what?

She couldn't bear the thought of going to the Laundry right now. She stepped out the back door of the main lodge, debating. Hemlocks and pines towered over her. Through their branches, she caught glimpses of stars dotting the inky sky. The dock. That's where she'd go. She needed fresh air and open water to relieve the stifling feelings compressing her heart.

Halfway down the path, she got a clear view of the dock. Doug sat there, his back toward her, feet dangling in the lake.

She paused. She was still wearing his shirt. He'd gone without one all afternoon till they got back to Pine Lodge.

"Mind if I join you?" she asked from a few feet behind him.

He glanced over his shoulder, then turned toward the lake again, shrugging. He seemed to be in a sullen mood. Of course, he'd had a very early morning, so he was probably just wiped. She hesitated, contemplating going back to the Laundry after all. But she wanted to be outside, and despite Janet's insinuations about his serious temper, he was the only person here she had any interest in talking to. She took off her shoes and sat beside him, dropping her feet in the cool water. Craning her neck, she gazed at the brilliant sky. "Wow."

"Yeah," he agreed. After a moment he added, "'And certain stars shot madly from their spheres.'"

"Shakespeare?"

He glanced at her, surprised. "You know it?"

She shook her head. "Lucky guess. Have you really read most of his plays?"

"A lot of them." He paused for a moment before adding, "I obviously had some time to kill."

She hesitated, wondering if he'd intentionally given her an opening to ask about his prison experience. "I guess that explains all your fancy vocabulary."

"What are you talking about?"

"Deign. Nefarious. Histrionic. That was all in my first five minutes of meeting you."

"Huh." He gave her an awkward smile. "I wasn't trying to impress you."

"Well, you did." She looked at him shyly. He was so handsome, in his brooding, mysterious way.

They sat in silence, their feet dangling in the water. Then he kicked his feet, rippling the water. "You should probably keep your feet moving a little, by the way."

"Why? If the fish want to nibble my toes, they won't hurt me."

"Snapping turtle."

Heidi pulled her feet onto the deck and looked at him in alarm. "You're joking, right?"

He shook his head. "I'm not actually. Big guy too. The other day I made the mistake of leaving some fish I'd caught dangling in the water. He—or she—was just finishing off the last one when I came to pull them out. Don't worry. I've never heard of anyone getting their toes snapped off. I just think it's probably a good idea to keep your feet moving."

"I'm never going in the water again."

"Sure you are. You're not prey."

She kept her feet on the dock. They sat in silence for a few minutes.

"You okay?" he finally asked. "I'm sorry about... all that, in the kitchen earlier."

"Not your fault, but thanks," Heidi said. She paused for a moment, staring at the dark water. Then she turned to him. "I have a proposal for you."

"Shoot."

"I won't Google you if you don't Google me."

He stared out over the water. "Do you mind telling me what Janet said to you?"

"She just said I should do my research... and, a little more."

He sighed. "Well, she's right. You should. Do your research."

"I'm not going to. If there's anything you want me to know about you, you tell me. Anything else is not my business."

"Unusual philosophy these days." He kicked his feet, making small waves in the water.

"Mrs. Hodges is my new hero. Not everyone would say that my tipping the canoe was a perfectly reasonable response to some catty questions. Even I think it was over the top."

He smiled. "Funny though. Yeah. Mrs. Hodges is pretty awesome. She hired me. I really appreciate that. I was having a bit of trouble finding a job."

She stayed silent, watching the rippling reflection of stars in the lake.

He cleared his throat. "I'll just tell you. I mean, it is all out there on the Internet. Even if you don't try to find out yourself, someone's going to tell you, so it may as well be me." He took a deep breath and exhaled. "Second-degree manslaughter. Involuntary. I got into a pretty brutal fistfight when I was eighteen. The guy died. I got out of prison six months ago."

Heidi felt a tinge of alarm. She had known it was possible, but now she knew for sure: she was sitting out here alone in the dark beside a man who had killed someone. A man who had spent years in prison because he had killed someone. She swallowed, unsure of what to say. Maybe she didn't want to know Doug any better. Maybe she should leave. She gave a quick side glance, then looked back again, letting her gaze linger.

This big lumberjack of a guy beside her was crying.

"Did you know him?" she asked hesitantly.

Doug nodded and swallowed. "He was my best friend," he said hoarsely.

Heidi didn't know what to say. Doug exuded misery. She was speechless in the presence of his obvious agony and regret. They sat together in silence. Moment after moment passed. He wiped his cheeks, as if irritated at himself.

"It was over a girl. It was so stupid. I'd do anything to be able to take it back. Anything to give him his life back. I wish it had been me."

"I'm sorry, Doug," she finally said. "I'm so sorry."

"Thanks."

"Who was the girl?"

"Her name was Trisha. I think she thought she was just flirting with both of us, but we both really liked her. And we were drinking. And we were stupid eighteen-year-old boys. He started the fight, hit me on the jaw. I hit him back really hard, and he fell and knocked his head on a cement stair. And he died, like, instantly." He shook his head, as if still disbelieving what had happened. He sighed again. "Anyway, Trisha, I think she was pretty traumatized. I never heard from her after that night. I can tell you, the whole nightmare definitely made me a bit skittish about developing feelings for anyone."

Hmm. That was an interesting admission. "Have you been involved with anyone since then?"

He shook his head.

Heidi put her feet back in the water and gently kicked back and forth. "Was prison hard?"

"Yes. Every minute of the day regulated by someone else. No privacy. Everyone around you angry, or depressed. When the guards felt like messing with you..." he shrugged. "They could. Who was going to stop them?"

"Did that happen often?"

He shook his head. "Most of them were okay. There are assholes in every group."

After a moment of silence, he continued, "The worst part was it was boring as hell. Except, you know, Shakespeare." He gave a bitter smile. "But honestly, I needed to know I was being punished. It may sound strange, but I was grateful for it. In a way, it's harder now because I get a new chance at life. And he'll never have that."

They sat in silence for a few minutes.

"What was his name?" Heidi asked.

"Ronnie. I wish I could talk to him again. Tell him how sorry I am."

"What do you think he'd say? If he were sitting here right now?"

Silence again. A long silence. She kept her eyes fixed on the water, but in her peripheral vision she saw him wiping tears off his face again.

"I'm so sorry," she whispered, grieving for him.

He shook his head. "I was just thinking—I could almost hear his voice."

"Saying what?"

"I felt like he was saying, 'Are you seriously going to be focusing on this when you've got such a pretty, and pretty awesome, girl sitting next to you?'" He glanced at Heidi. "Sorry. That's just the kind of thing he would say, though."

"So, you think he'd forgive you? Maybe has forgiven you?"

"I hope so." Tears streamed down his face. "Man, I am so sorry," he said, wiping them away with his shirt. "Haven't cried in a while. I'm a real mess tonight. Don't know what's gotten into me."

"It's okay. I don't mind. I won't tell anyone."

"Yeah, I guess I trust that."

"Ben and Harry said they've known you a long time."

He nodded. "My family used to come here for vacation. Two weeks every summer. Ronnie always came with us. Harry and Ben were a few years younger, but we let them hang around with us. They were like these adoring little brothers. We had a blast. Played a game called *King of the Raft,* which basically involved pushing each other off that raft out there."

He jutted his chin toward the floating raft about ten yards from the dock. He grinned, remembering. Then his smile faded. "Anyway. They were really great while I was away. Both Harry and Ben. They wrote me letters." He cleared his throat. "It meant a lot. I mean, you find out who your friends are, that's for sure. And when I got out, they talked to their grandmother. That's why I'm here."

"Thanks for sharing all that with me. I'm really sorry. It's such a horrible tragedy."

He nodded. "Yeah. Anyway, whatever your big secret is, I don't think you can top mine. I'm not prying, just giving you some perspective."

She shrugged. "Well, you're right, it doesn't top yours, but in the town that I lived in, you wouldn't know the difference." She hesitated for a moment. But he had trusted her. She chose to trust him. "There was this boy I'd dated since high school. Nine years. Everyone thought we were the perfect couple.

"Or at least, they thought I was lucky to be the girl he chose. He could have had his pick. He was handsome and smart and athletic and fun, and everyone thought he was the nicest guy in the world. And he seemed to adore me. Always wanted me to be with him. Wanted me to go to the same college with him, so I did. Wanted me working at his family's firm with him after college, so I did. My parents thought I hit the boyfriend jackpot. But...." She cringed and swallowed. "I don't want you to think I'm a horrible person, but I'm afraid you're going to."

He didn't look at her, but she could tell he was listening intently. "I doubt that," he said quietly.

"Well, I feel like a horrible person. But the truth is, I was bored. I felt... stifled." She stopped, overcome with self-consciousness. This grown man had just been sobbing in front of her, relating something in his life that she would never be able to fathom, and she was blathering on about what to him must seem like nothing. "Sorry, Doug," she said. "This is pure small-town soap opera compared to what you've done—um—what you've been through."

He looked over at her, clear-eyed and in control of himself again. "No, Heidi. It happened to you, so I'm interested. If you want to tell me, I'd like to know."

She felt like a stone had dislodged in her throat. Here was

someone who would not judge her or use her story for idle gossip. At least, she hoped so, enough to risk telling him. "A few times over the years, I tried to break things off, but he freaked out. He told me how much he loved me and said we had something so special and please don't break his heart. And I thought I was crazy not to appreciate that I had a smart, caring, handsome man wanting to be with me. Both our families loved that we were together. His parents thought I was the girl next door, down-to-earth, level-headed, yada, yada. My parents considered him their dream son-in-law, clean-cut Mr. Perfect.

"Anyway, every time, I just gave in and didn't break up with him. Things would be fine for a while until I felt like I couldn't breathe again. I'd suggest we take a little time apart, and he'd freak out again, and I'd give in again. Kept trying to convince myself that at some point I'd realize what a good deal I had with him.

"And then he proposed to me. At a baseball game. On camera. In front of a gazillion people. I was so pissed off." She shook her head, feeling the anger rise in her chest all over again. "I played the part—I cried, I accepted, I kissed him, I put the ring on. But I felt so manipulated. I think he knew if he'd proposed when we were alone somewhere, I would have turned him down—or at least put it off.

"So, people in town started putting on engagement parties for us. And I started to realize it was really going to happen. I was going to marry him. Everyone was congratulating me, and I just felt trapped. Well, one night, one of his out-of-town cousins came to one of the parties. He was cute, and I got drunk...." She took a deep breath and exhaled slowly. "And I slept with him. I'd never done anything like that before. I'd never even been drunk before. That's what a good girl I was."

She waited for Doug to comment on this, but he said nothing. He didn't look at her either. He just seemed to be listening, waiting.

"So, that was horrid of me, of course, and I felt very ashamed, and I knew I had to tell Alan," she continued. "But, before I could do that, at a brunch the next day, the cousin made this big public apology to Alan in front of about thirty people, and said,"—here she imitated the man's deep voice—"'Alan, I don't think this is the girl that you should marry. She's a slut!'"

Doug made an inarticulate grumble in his throat. He continued to stare out over the lake. She waited for more of a response from him. Finally, he said, "Go on."

"My fiancé was devastated, of course. He hated me from that moment on, and I don't blame him. It was a horrible thing to do, and he felt totally humiliated." She gave a short laugh. "Though he got over it pretty fast. He's already married to another class-mate. Neither one of them will acknowledge my existence. Both our families were furious with me, and his family was furious with mine, breaking a decades-long friendship. I became the town pariah. I had to take down all my social media because people were so hateful. It was ugly."

She sighed and clasped her hands together in her lap. "And the craziest thing is, despite all that, all I could feel was this intense relief that I'd gotten out of the trap I was in." She leaned back on her arms and looked up at the star-studded sky. "Anyway, there you have it. The whole sordid story. What you did was a tragic accident, but I'm basically an awful person."

He gave her a swift, incredulous look. "Are you kidding me? The guy didn't listen to you. Sounds like a manipulative prick to me. He got what he deserved. It just stinks that everyone in town took his side."

"Yeah. I got pretty much branded a heartbreaking slut."

"That sucks. Doesn't make it true, though."

"But it was a horrible thing to do. And he really was a nice guy."

He turned to her and held her gaze. "Don't kid yourself, Heidi. If he was a nice guy, you would have been able to have honest conversations, and he'd have been able to hear you say you wanted out and respected you enough to call it quits. And he'd be able to get over all that shit by now and talk to you like a normal person and realize he had some part in it, too. If he was a nice guy, he would care about you enough to not want the whole community to shun you or be nasty to you. I'm not saying you shouldn't have been able to break it off without sleeping with another guy, but he didn't make it easy. This does not, in any way, make you a horrible person. Stop feeling guilty about it. Seriously. I absolve you."

Heidi turned her eyes on the water, but she couldn't keep the smile off her face. This was the very first time anyone had suggested that the whole relationship implosion and its ugly aftermath had not been entirely her fault. It felt so refreshing. She had a hopeful feeling about Doug. She needed a friend right now. He could be a friend. Maybe more.

"Thanks," she said. "I want to believe you."

"Believe me," he said. "Is that why you blushed so hard in the kitchen earlier? Because you were ashamed of sleeping with the cousin?"

She nodded.

"Sounds like a whole family of assholes to me," he said. "Good riddance."

She laughed. "Oh, my God. I feel so much better. I just... thank you, Doug. Really. Thank you."

He looked at her contemplatively.

"It's getting chilly," she said.

He stood up and took off his shirt.

"What are you doing?"

"Going swimming. Come on."

"The water's freezing."

"Warmer than the air. It'll be invigorating." He dropped his shorts and dove into the lake, wearing only his boxers.

She grinned and stood. Slipping out of her shorts and his big tee shirt, she dove in after him, following him to the raft. He waited for her, holding onto the wooden ladder.

"It's invigorating, all right," she said, clasping the ladder. "But now I don't want to get out. The air will be too cold."

He grinned at her. "I don't want to get out either." His face glistened in the starlight, water droplets sparkling on his beard. She moved closer to him. He looked scared, like she felt. Yet, he looked hopeful, too.

"So, Heidi," he said. "I was wondering what you might think about kissing a sad, lonely-as-shit-ex-con."

"I'm lonely too." She let her leg brush against his under water. "Are you feeling skittish?"

He smiled at her and shook his head. "I'm not, actually. You?"

"I'm not either."

His arm encircled her waist and drew her close, his gaze tender and shy, full of longing and hope. She slid her arms around his neck.

"All right, then," he said. And he kissed her.

1

AN EX CHECKS IN

Joe's checking up on me. He always worries I'm going to get tired driving. Plus, this is the first high school reunion I've attended without him at my side. I think we're both sad about it. I know I am.

I press my car speakerphone and answer all the questions I know are coming: "I'm still on the thruway. Ten miles from Albany. Two hours to go. Traffic isn't terrible. I'm not tired."

"I'm not checking up on you," he says defensively. "I can't find my files for my presentation on Monday. I've looked everywhere, in all those folders you made for me."

"What name did you save it under?"

"I don't remember. But I know you can find it. It's the one dated from this morning."

I groan. For a brilliant college chemistry professor, Joe is an idiot when it comes to some of life's more fundamental skills.

"Joe, I'm in the car. I can't help you. Ask Fiona." Our daughter lives in the second bedroom of Joe and Annie's Upper East Side apartment these days and works from home, so I know she's around.

"I did ask her, but she said she's on strike. She says she's explained it too many times."

"So have I. Come on, Joe. Ask Annie, for goodness' sake."

A long pause. "Annie's never considered clerical support part of our marital contract."

Clerical support. I grit my teeth. How did I stay married to this man for nearly twenty years? How am I still friends with him, despite his falling in love with another woman? Why the hell am I proud of Annie for refusing to get sucked into his charming incompetence? I never wanted to like the woman who broke up my marriage, but I can't help it. She's a delightful conversationalist, nonjudgmental, and shares his fascination for all things chemistry.

"Figure it out, Joe. Was there anything else? Get off my tail, asshole," I snap at the driver behind me.

"Get out of the fast lane," Joe says.

"I'm going the speed limit."

"I know, and that's pissing off the driver behind you because you're in the fast lane. Have some consideration for your fellow drivers, Gretchen."

I put on my blinker and move out of the fast lane. The Ford Explorer roars past me, making a point. I don't understand why people have such attitudes against drivers who simply follow the rules and go the speed limit.

"Looking forward to the reunion?"

Ah, the real reason he'd called. "Yes. Do you wish you were going?"

"Kind of," he says, surprising me with his honesty. "First I've missed."

"The second," I say. "We both missed my twenty-fifth." The last thing I'd wanted to do five years ago was show up to that and tell everyone that my charming and gregarious husband, who had been so popular at these events that some classmates mistakenly assumed he'd graduated with us, had left me for another chemistry professor in his department.

An awkward moment of silence passes.

"So, who's going to be there?"

"Lena, Anne-Marie, Sophia." The Rock Lobsters, my friend group from seventh grade on. "Queenie. Eva and Lori." Friends I'd made at reunions post high school.

"Any guys?"

I smile, glad he can't see my face. "Well, Brad Atkinson has signed up."

My heart gives a flutter, just saying his name out loud. Brad Atkinson, my crush since fourth grade, and our high school football team captain, voted by the class as "Most Likely to Succeed," which has certainly borne out, given the way he buys and sells companies like he's still a little kid winning Monopoly games. Brad was also the reason Joe proposed to me on the drive home after the first weekend I brought him to Warren to introduce him to my family and friends. Later, after we were married, Joe admitted he'd felt a little competition that weekend and decided to move fast. I was flattered to think Joe saw me as a woman men might compete over, but Brad had been no competition for Joe, at the time.

Times have changed. Joe isn't worried about competition for my affections and I'm more than a little interested in rekindling some of the romantic energy that used to exist between me and Brad. I'm sure I'm not the only woman looking forward to catching up with him, but I hope I'm the only woman he's sending flirty emails to.

"Do you seriously still have a crush on Brad Atkinson?" Joe sounds surprised and slightly amused. "Yeah, yeah, I know he looks like Brad Pitt and is some hotshot Fortune 500 dude with houses on three continents."

My eyes widen. "How do you even know anything about his

work or how many houses he has? I could not tell you a single thing about any of your high school classmates, even though I went to all your reunions, too. How do you retain all this information?"

"Brilliant. You know that."

"Except when it comes to finding your computer files."

"That's not important to remember. I can always ask you."

He's not teasing. If I were looking right at him, I'd see him saying that with a straight face. I thought I was going to be free of his dependencies once we got divorced, but here I am, six years later, still helping him with those basic administrative skills that are too unimportant for him to learn for himself and that his current wife won't take on.

"What about that guy, your old friend, the lab partner? Vic, right?"

My throat tightens. I swallow. "Right." A hollow spot in my chest expands, causing a dull ache. Vic, my lab partner for ninth-grade earth science, tenth-grade biology, eleventh-grade chemistry, and twelfth-grade physics, and the reason I maintained a decent class rank because sciences were so not my thing. "He hasn't signed up."

I sense Joe wanting to ask a question, but he doesn't. He waits me out.

"I can't believe you even remember him," I say. "He hasn't been to any reunions."

"Sure, I remember him. I met him when I met all the rest of your friends. He was planning to teach chemistry."

I smile. "Well, of course you'd remember that." My smile fades away.

"Did he? Teach chemistry?"

"I have no idea."

"Really?" he questions, a tinge of skepticism in his voice.

What in the world is making Joe ask about Vic, someone he

only met once another lifetime ago? I don't want to think about Vic. Though I do happen to know that he's a chemistry teacher living in Seattle with his wife. I used to stalk him, but I made myself stop that years ago. There's no point in spending mental energy on someone who used to be your friend and isn't anymore.

"Yes, really," I insist, irritated. "He disappeared and was never heard from again. I don't know anything about him, Joe," I snap. "Stop honking at me!" I shout at the driver behind me.

"Gretchen, are you in the fast lane again?" Joe asks.

I am. How did that happen? I put on my blinker and change lanes. A Tesla passes me, the man in the passenger seat giving me the finger. I know better than to complain about that to Joe. He would consider that man's inexcusable rudeness entirely my fault.

"I bet Brad Atkinson can find his own computer files," I say, deliberately changing to a more cheerful topic of conversation.

Joe gives an amused laugh. "If that's a quality that's attractive to you, then have fun with the guy." *Thanks so much for the permission, Joe.* "Just don't marry him. His track record sucks."

"How's my track record?" I ask.

"Hey, our divorce didn't make any headlines. His divorces all made headlines. Just saying. Anyway, send my greetings to anyone who doesn't hate me."

He sounds sad, but I don't let myself feel sorry for him. There are consequences for one's actions, after all. Lena still rolls her eyes whenever I mention Joe. She can't believe we're friends. To her, infidelity is unforgivable. I think infidelity sucks, but on the spectrum of infidelities, truly falling in love with someone else while still caring deeply for your spouse... well, I suppose, from my perspective, that's not unforgivable. I forgave Joe, anyway, and I'm glad I did. On this matter, Lena and I have agreed to disagree.

"Give my love to Fiona and say hi to Annie for me."

"Will do. Drive safe. Have fun this weekend."

"I'm planning to." I smile, half expecting him to give me another warning about Brad, but he doesn't, for which I'm grateful. I haven't had a decent date or any kind of fling in years. Since before I was married to Joe, come to think of it. Those emails from Brad have been lifting my spirits. I'm excited to see him again.

2

THE PROM KISS KISS-OFF

Two hours later, I exit the thruway and within twenty minutes arrive in the village of Warren, where I grew up. I pull into my parents' gravel driveway, and they immediately come out the back door to greet me. They're in their late seventies now and I'm surprised to see my dad using a cane and looking more stooped than he did at Christmas. My mother, however, appears as strong and wiry as ever, her formerly blonde hair now an elegant white. She embraces me in a brief, warm hug.

"Didn't the reunion start at six?" She grabs one of my tote bags and pushes me into the house. "You're going to be late for the cocktail hour, Gretchen. I'm so glad you let your hair go back to its natural color."

"You mean you're so glad I took advantage of the miracle of chemistry to achieve this lovely brown with blonde highlights instead of letting my gray show?" I bat my eyelashes at her.

"By the way," my mother continues, ignoring me. Her eyes have lit up. "You'll never guess who dropped by the house to say hello and see if you were here yet."

"Lena?" She always makes a point of seeing my parents when she's in town.

"Well of course Lena, that was nice of her, but no, I meant Brad Atkinson! And he's as handsome as he ever was. I always liked Brad."

I can't hide my grin. My mother eyes me intently, biting back her curiosity.

I run upstairs, take a quick shower, comb my hair, leaving it loose around my shoulders, and change into a pink, retro, sleeveless shift dress. I might not have as much right to bare arms as Michelle Obama, but I keep up my swimming and strength training and Fiona, my twenty-one-year-old fashion guide, has approved my wardrobe for the weekend. Sliding into my flat sandals, I run downstairs. "Love you, Mom and Dad," I say as I dash through the kitchen.

"What time will you be in?" my father asks.

"I don't know. Don't wait up." I say this knowing perfectly well he'll be waiting up, even though his baby girl is now forty-eight-years old.

Fresh July air wafts through my open window as I drive through Warren's rolling hills toward the Shady Spring Country Club on the peak of Henderson Hill. Every five years since we graduated, our reunions have begun with a cocktail party and a Friday night dinner at the Country Club. Brad, Lena, and Sophia are all on the Alumni Relations Committee. I'm sure that has something to do with it.

I've always had mixed feelings about the Country Club. In high school, kids fell into different categories depending on their relationship to the club.

There were families like Brad's and Lena's and Sophia's who were members, whose kids spent the whole summer there swimming and golfing and playing tennis.

There were families like mine and Anne-Marie's, who were friends with people who had memberships. Anne-Marie and I could go to the club's outdoor pool a certain number of times each summer, five times as Lena's guest and five times as Sophia's. And starting in middle school, I joined the school swim team, and we had our practices and meets in the indoor pool, so I was familiar with the club's interior space too.

Then there were families like Vic's, who swam in the town pool, which looked pretty rundown in comparison, clumps of grass growing through cracks in the pavement and rust on the chain-link fences. Vic was a strong swimmer and a summer lifeguard for the town pool during high school. I think he would have loved to be on the school swim team, but he couldn't give up every Saturday for meets because he had to work in his parents' lumberyard. The only times he ever went to the Country Club were when they needed a substitute lifeguard or as part of a catering crew for special events. If there was a job to be had in Warren, Vic had done it.

And then there were families we used to call the Trailers, families like Queenie's. I cringe now at how we didn't think anything of labeling people by where they lived, though Queenie and her friends owned the label like a badge of pride. At our fifth reunion, the first time Queenie and I ever really talked to each other, she looked around the elegant veranda, with its white latticework and view of the golf course's rolling hills, her eyes wide with amazement. I said, "I know how you feel. I have to remind myself that I don't need to explain to anyone here whose guest I am tonight." Queenie responded, "Girl, you have no idea how I feel. I never in my life thought I'd step foot in this place."

That was awkward. But the awkwardness dissipated over the years, along with other barriers. In high school, the Brains,

Jocks, Artists, Goths, Druggies, Trailers, and Loners rarely spoke to anyone outside their clique, though Lena, Brad, Vic, and I, being Brains and Jocks, had a bit more social fluidity than most. By the fifth reunion, however, the clique walls began to crumble. By the tenth one, thanks to the outreach of the Jocks and Artists and Trailers, who all turned out to have a lot of class spirit and energy to put into planning reunions, it no longer mattered what groups we'd been in.

The parking lot has filled up by the time I arrive, but I find a spot. I turn off the car and pause, feeling a tinge of nervousness. I haven't seen most of these people for ten years and my life has changed so much from the last time I was here. I've studied my classmates' faces on Facebook and memorized the registration list, not wanting to embarrass myself by not recognizing anyone. I tried to dig up my old yearbook too, but I don't know where in the world I've packed that away. People are gathering on the veranda out back, but I decide to go to the restroom first.

Entering the club through the front double doors, I peek into the dining room. Under a massive chandelier, waitstaff scurries around circular tables for eight, beautifully set with white tablecloths, gleaming silverware, and peony centerpieces, putting final touches on the decorations.

I make my way down the wide corridor and stop, stunned to see a display of photos from high school that have been blown up in color prints lining the corridors' walls. Someone spent an extraordinary amount of time putting together this trip down memory lane. First up are the class pictures from kindergarten through twelfth grade. I'm the tallest kid in every class through middle school. I remember the relief I felt the first day of ninth grade, discovering that the boys had finally, finally shot up and were taller than me.

I progress slowly down the hall, looking for photos of myself and my friends, of course. There I am with the swim team, in my maroon one-piece swimsuit, cap, and goggles. There's Brad with the football team, holding up a championship trophy. There's Anne-Marie and Sophia wearing gingham dresses for the twelfth-grade production of *Oklahoma!* There's Lena, giving her speech as valedictorian.

And there are the prom pictures. I want to walk by without looking, but of course, I don't. I scan the wall for the group photo I know will be there in the mix and there it is: me and Vic, Brad and Alecia, Lena, Sophia, and their dates—the boys in black tuxes, the girls in long, flowing dresses. Mine was blue, strapless, sparkly. I loved that dress.

I don't want the memories of that night to crash over me, but they do anyway.

A week before prom, I still didn't have a date, and I was desperate. I'd been so sure that either Brad or Vic would ask me that I'd turned down offers from guys on the swim team. They'd both promised to ask me, after all, though that had been in fourth grade, and I was mortified to realize neither of them remembered. And it turned out that in twelfth grade, they were the only two boys I wanted to go with, Brad because I'd always had a crush on him, and Vic because he was one of my best friends and I assumed he'd be my date if Brad wasn't.

After Brad asked Alecia, Vic, to my horror, still didn't ask me. Nor did he ask any of the other girls besides me who would have been delighted to be his date. He was not as flashy as Brad, but he was a stud in his own quiet, lifeguard/ lab coat/ weekend lumberyard-worker way, and he was one of my best friends. I ended up having to beg him to go with me. He tried to talk me into an all-night *Star Wars* marathon instead. As an adult, I've come to suspect his reluctance was because of the money it cost him—renting a tux, taking me out for a fancy dinner, renting the limo. It never crossed my mind to contribute, even though I'd been the one to ask him to the prom.

Was there an expiration date on feeling bad about mistakes one made in the past, or was I going to be burdened with guilt about my clueless insensitivity as a seventeen-year-old for the rest of my life?

Gazing at the photo of our young, smiling faces, I can't help but smile back at my teenage self. We had a wonderful prom night, Vic and I. Except for that one mortifying moment when I tried to kiss him. One minute, we were taking a break from dancing, the next minute, I was gazing into his laughing hazel eyes and had what felt like an epiphany: whatever we might tell ourselves, Vic and I were more than friends. I wanted to kiss him. I wanted to do much more than kiss him. I wanted him to be my first lover. And the way Vic was looking at me, I felt certain he wanted me, too.

Pressing a hand against my heart, I close my eyes. I've relived that cringe-worthy moment over and over, stopping mid-walk even years later, even up to this moment, to blush with shame at the memory of sliding my arms around his waist, lifting my face toward his, closing my eyes, and then feeling his hands on my hips as he roughly pushed me away from him and said, "I'm not letting you use me to make Brad jealous." I protested that I absolutely had not been thinking about Brad at that moment, but Vic didn't believe me. I could still hear his stern rebuke: "Don't do that again."

We stared at each other. I wanted a suction hole to appear in the gym floor and vacuum me away. I turned away from him so he wouldn't see the tears brimming in my eyes. I would have wiped them away, but I didn't want to smear the eye makeup I'd applied so carefully. Each moment of silence between us seemed like an hour. But then Vic, ever kind, turned me to face him. He took a handkerchief from his pocket and blotted the tears on my face. Then he put an arm around my shoulder and moved me toward the dance floor, saying, "Friends, Gretchen?"

To him, I said, "Of course, Vic," and to myself I said, "Oh, don't worry, I will never do that again." I'd learned my lesson: we were just friends.

Oh, Vic, where did you go?

I squeeze my eyes shut, then open them and force myself to walk down the corridor without looking at any more photos. I enter the women's room, relieved to find it empty, and flop down on a flowery blue ottoman. My heart is still racing. I make myself take deep breaths.

Was I right to come back or should I have skipped this reunion, too? Why do I suddenly feel so anxious about seeing people again? Am I afraid I won't measure up? There's no reason I should be. I've always been popular enough. And I've had a successful career working in social services, the last fifteen years as director of a residence for senior citizens living with chronic mental illness and histories of homelessness. I'm the mother of two young adults, of whom I'm immensely proud.

Of course, I never expected to be divorced at forty-two, or to find myself at forty-eight, embarrassingly grateful for my ex-husband's friendship and afraid of being alone for the next chapter of my life.

I straighten up. I'm also someone who's kept her best friends from seventh grade. And I'm a woman that Brad Atkinson has been sending sweet, funny emails to. I'm so glad Brad is still my friend, that he's made a point of keeping up with me over the years. I know my friendship means something to him. I'm not fooling myself that it's anything more than that: I'm not looking for love this weekend. I'm not in the market for another husband, either. But some fun, some flirting, perhaps a fling? I'm up for that.

I stand, put on another coat of coral lipstick, blot my lips on a tissue, give myself one last look, then leave the bathroom and exit the clubhouse by a side door.

Walking around a putting green on the west side of the clubhouse, I head toward the back veranda where a sizable crowd has gathered. My classmates wear a variety of interpretations of business casual. Some people look virtually unchanged from high school, while others are unrecognizable, especially the men who sport less hair and more girth.

I search the crowd for Lena, but while I don't locate her right away, I do see a face I recognize. Molly Mark, the former class president and current Reunion Committee Chair, stands by the Welcome Table, a clipboard pressed to her chest. If I remember correctly, Molly was voted "Most Likely to Tell You Exactly What She's Thinking." I smile and head her way, girding myself for an earful.

"Hello, Gretchen!" she squeals, handing me a name tag. "So glad you could make it." She leans toward me, and I smell rum on her breath. "We missed you at the twenty-fifth. I'm so glad we're still all coming back for these, and I must say, we women are looking pretty darn well-preserved!" Molly giggles. "I'm divorced too, now, by the way. Don't ask. It wasn't pretty. There are quite a few of us divorced this time. Including Brad Atkinson —again—did you hear? Oh, of course, you two probably keep up, don't you?"

She watches my face, obviously prying. I nod, affecting nonchalance.

"Well, I met his most recent ex at the twenty-fifth and I could have told you right then it wasn't going to last. She was too clingy. Know what I mean? He was just being his usual friendly self, but it was so obvious it bothered her. So, he's newly available, not that any of us care about that, right? I mean, who cares about a house in Barbados, right?" She giggles again. "But, man, oh man, has he kept his looks. You can't say that about all the guys."

I follow her gaze toward a group of men standing about the lawn. There's Brad, a head taller than most of the guys who circle around him. His throaty laugh carries over the other men's voices. It's been ten years since I've seen him in person. He is still a fine male specimen, broad-shouldered, athletic, and fit as ever, a full head of blond hair just a bit whiter than it used to be, a shiny gold watch on his wrist. Lena will tell me later how much it costs. Just what you'd expect Mr. "Most Likely to Succeed" to look like at his thirtieth reunion.

But his wealth or his jock status isn't what draws me to him. He's always made me feel special. There's a connection between us. There always has been. One night, when we were on a break from college and he was kissing me on the golf course under the stars, Brad said that someday, when the stars align, I might just find him on bended knee, sliding a ring on my finger. I knew it was probably a toss-off line for him, something he probably said to a lot of girls, given his "track record." But for me, it was one of the most romantic moments of my life.

At that moment, Brad turns toward me, and we lock eyes. He winks. I smile. We hold each other's gaze for a long moment. Then he gives me that gorgeous smile and nods, jutting out his chin, indicating he'll be coming to find me later. I know how to read his signals. It's like no time at all has passed since the last time we silently communicated that sometime soon we'd be sneaking off together somewhere, though it has in fact been nearly three decades since that happened.

"Ooh," coos Molly. "There always was something electric between you two, wasn't there? And still there, after all these years."

I shrug, giving her a closed-mouth smile. Molly is the last person I plan to share any of my fantasies with. Over her shoul-

der, I finally spot my friends across the veranda, waving at me.
"Oh look, there's Lena."

"Go, have fun," Molly says.

"Lovely to see you again." We exchange air kisses.

"We'll catch up more later!"

"Of course," I say, though that is all the catching up I needed
to do with Molly Mark this weekend.

3

FOOTSIE BY THE FIR TREES

A moment later, the Rock Lobsters—Lena, Anne-Marie, Sophia, and I—enfold each other in a four-way, warm, slightly sweaty embrace.

"Rock Lobster!" we all whisper in our huddle. The B-52s' hit has been our theme song since we were twelve-year-old girls. I know so many people who haven't kept up with anyone from high school, but from seventh grade on, I won the friend lottery. The four of us see each other in between reunions, more so now that our children are older, so we don't have too much we need to catch up on.

"Tonight, we mingle. Tomorrow, breakfast at the Village Café, 9AM sharp," Lena says.

"Be there, or B-52," the three of us respond in unison, then burst into laughter. Having our small group together again warms my heart. Honestly, I think, not for the first time, when it really comes down to it, as long as a woman has her friends, who needs men?

"Who are you planning to catch up with first?" Lena asks me after Sophia and Anne-Marie take off. "Brad Atkinson, by any chance?"

"Queenie," I say, nodding toward the lawn where she stands with her two best friends, Lori and Eva. Queenie runs a halfway house for young adults who've aged out of the foster care system. We always have a lot to talk about, picking each other's brains about best practices, sharing some of the more hair-raising situations we've dealt with, which only another person who works with at-risk populations would understand.

"Of course," Lena says. "Have fun tonight." We squeeze hands and let each other go.

Queenie waves me over. I cross the grass, grateful for my flat sandals, and give her a hug. Lori and Eva both smile at me but don't stop their conversation.

"There absolutely is room for another book group at the library," Eva says to Lori. "They have historical fiction, nonfiction, literary fiction, and science fiction book groups. There's no reason they shouldn't agree to a romance book group, too."

"I'd just prefer a fantasy book group," Lori says. "If they're only going to add one more, then that's what I'd like to advocate for."

"Join the science fiction group with Queenie," Eva says.

"It's not the same thing at all as you would know if you read either genre."

Eva shakes her head. "Nope. I'm only interested in happy endings, and I don't like dragons in my stories either."

Queenie laughs. "You two! Just go tell them you're going to start a romance book group and a fantasy book group. They'll be thrilled, as long as you agree to run the groups yourselves."

"Oh, my God, look at Gretchen's face," Lori exclaims to the others with a mischievous grin. "Remember when the Brains thought none of the Trailers could read?"

Heat rushes to my cheeks. "I'm so sorry if I was a snob in high school."

"Oh, stop it, Lori." Queenie reaches up to link her arm

through mine. We make quite the pair—I, tall, fair-skinned, in a pink sheath and flats, she, short, dark-skinned, in a sexy black cocktail dress and three-inch platform sandals. "Gretchen was always one of the nice Brains. Don't tease her."

"I thought Gretchen was a Jock." Eva wrinkles her brow. "Swim team, right?"

"Weren't all the Rock Lobsters Brains?" Lori asks me.

"Who cares now?" Queenie says, putting her free hand on her hip and looking imposing.

Lori smiles at me. "That's right. None of us can help where we got pigeon-holed. And you were one of the nice snobs back then. We're nice to everyone now. But we remember." The three of them raise their eyebrows at each other, nodding in unspoken communication.

We chat some more. They all still live in Warren, though Queenie and Eva no longer live in the trailer park where they grew up. Eva's a receptionist at the elementary school, and Lori manages that trailer park and oversees a strong, vibrant community there.

It amazes me, and makes me more than a little sad, that in high school we hardly spoke a word to each other. Given how well we get on now, we really could have been friends. But our lives were so different, then. All three of them had babies or toddlers in their arms at our high school graduation, and I absorbed all my parents' dire predictions about their futures. My parents used to plead with me, at length, not to ruin my life by getting pregnant. This was something they had to worry about a lot less than they thought they did, as I didn't become sexually active till college, but I didn't tell them that. And, as it turned out, none of these women ruined their lives, either.

I shake my head, blinking, and look at Queenie, who's laughing at me.

"Still having your space-out moments, I see," she says. "Sit with us. Unless you made plans to eat with the Rock Lobsters?"

"No, we're having breakfast tomorrow," I say. "I'd love to join you." I glance across the lawn and catch Brad's eye. He winks again, excuses himself to the group he's with, and backs away, heading west toward the putting green, his gaze holding mine. Something inside me feels like a giggly teenager again.

"You sure you're not going to want to eat with Brad?" Queenie asks.

"I'm sure," I say. "I'm going to catch up with him for a bit right now, but then I'll find you, so save me a seat."

Brad waits on the far side of the putting green with his hands on his hips, watching me with apparent pleasure, his eyes skating up and down my body as I approach. Then he spreads his arms, and I step into his warm embrace. It has been such a long time since any man has held me like this, with a hug that means friendship, and perhaps more. He kisses my cheek, his lips lingering a little longer than necessary, then takes a step back to look at me. And here I am, on this balmy July evening in the very romantic setting that I've been fantasizing about with the very man who's been appearing in those fantasies for the past four months.

"It's so good to see you, Gretchen. Honest to God, you look exactly the same as you did in high school. Gorgeous as ever."

"Exactly the same, only thirty years older." I don't mind the compliments. Joe was never one for verbal affirmations. His "love language" was acts of service. I never minded doing things for him, providing that extra bit of "clerical support" as he calls it, because I knew he truly appreciated it, that it made him feel loved. But I would have appreciated hearing him tell me on occasion that he liked how I looked, the way Brad was doing now. My soul feels parched for whispers of sweet nothings. "Shall we walk a little?" I suggest.

He grins, sliding an arm around my shoulder and points to a small copse of fir trees behind which sits a little wrought-iron bench we know well, though it's been decades since we sat there together. "Our old spot?" he asks.

I nod, not caring if people notice or if they talk. I hunger for the physical and emotional warmth Brad offers me. We stroll away from our classmates, make our way behind the trees to the bench, and sit down, close enough for our thighs to touch. He keeps his arm around my shoulder, and I reach up and clasp his fingers. We have a perfect view of the third hole, where two men in plaid golf shorts are making their way to the green.

"You seem sad, Gretchen," Brad says.

I shrug, smiling. "Do I? I feel happy, I think. Glad to see you."

"Likewise. So, how are you? I hope your divorce was a little less hellacious than mine."

"I'm sure it was," I say. "Not easy, of course. I'm not going to lie and say Joe didn't break my heart, because he did, but somehow, his determination to salvage our friendship softened the heartbreak."

He nods. "You have kids, so I understand trying to be cordial for their sake."

I shake my head. "It's not just that. We're actually friends."

Brad gives me a skeptical side eye, but when I hold his gaze, he says, "Well, good for you. I can't imagine it with any of my exes. And I'm not going to lie to you and say I'm sorry you're not still with Joe. He and I never really hit it off at these reunions. I guess two alpha males in a group tend to make things uncomfortable for everyone."

"Oh, yes," I say, keeping a straight face. "It's terribly uncomfortable for the rest of us when we find ourselves in a group with two alpha males."

He laughs. "Aren't you glad my ego's still intact?"

"Yes." I smile. "So, how is work in the world of mergers and acquisitions?"

Brad squeezes my shoulder. "Ah, Gretchen. You really want to catch up with me. I love that about you. Part of me thought you'd just want a little make-out session for old time's sake."

I raise my eyebrow at him. Am I that obvious?

He laughs. "Come on. It's me. You don't need to play games. I'm just touched to know it's not all you want." His phone vibrates. With a grimace, he takes it out of his pocket, glances at the message, and puts it away again. "Sorry."

"Of course, that's not all I want." I press my knee into his and he presses back. "I care about you. It means a lot to me that you've made an effort to stay in touch with me all these years. I can't say that about everyone, that's for sure." I turn to face him, looking right into his blue eyes. We hold each other's gaze. His lips are inches from mine.

"You're a special woman, Gretchen Holloway. Why didn't we ever go all the way?" He narrows his eyes. "We didn't, did we?"

I huff and pull away from him, folding my arms across my chest.

He laughs again, raising his hands in mock terror. "I'm an asshole. Of course we didn't because I would one hundred percent remember it if we had." He peers at me with a slightly anxious look, and I have the unsettling suspicion that he wants confirmation on this matter. Clearly, what our romantic interludes together meant to me and what they meant to him differed dramatically. "So, same question," he persists. "Why didn't we? I always wanted you."

My cheeks grow warm. "Well, you were usually dating someone and however much you wanted me, I don't think you wanted to go out with me. You didn't, for example, ask me to prom. So, we just had those little bits of time in between your other relationships, and that window was never very wide. That's why."

"I should have dated you." Brad sighs, a somber expression on his handsome face. He looks out over the golf course's verdant, rolling hills, where the setting sun sinks into ribbons of violet and orange. "Maybe my life would have turned out better in the love department if I'd let myself fall in love with someone sensible and down-to-earth."

"Oh, God," I groan. "Gorgeous was fine. Stick with gorgeous."

Brad throws back his head and laughs. "You are gorgeous. And sensible and down-to-earth, and all of that is wonderful. I don't know why I always had to fall for the damn drama queens."

"Mergers and acquisitions, Brad," I say.

"Ah, yes," he whispers into my ear. "Don't let me get side-tracked."

I let myself lean into him and he slides his arm back around my shoulder. I hesitate, then let my fingers land on his thigh. He murmurs appreciatively and nuzzles my neck.

His phone vibrates again. He pulls out his phone again to read the message, shoves it back in his pocket, and jiggles my foot with his shoe. Footsie by the fir trees. I've missed his playfulness.

"I love my work," he says. "It's the one part of my life I have no regrets about. I really, really like making deals, negotiating, and ultimately, making money, of course. Don't think less of me, please. At least I'm honest about it, right?"

I nod. "Honesty rocks."

"Remind me what you do again? Nursing, was it?"

I shake my head, not surprised he doesn't remember. "Social work. I'm the director of a residence for people living with chronic mental illness who have histories of homelessness."

"God, that sounds like hell." He pushes a hand through his blond-white hair, shaking his head in disbelief. "How do you do it? It must be the most depressing work ever."

"It's not depressing at all. I love what I do. It's incredible how resilient people can be in the face of... just... unimaginable challenges. I'm inspired every day. And I feel like, at least in little ways, I make a difference. It's community building, really, with the residents, with the neighborhood." I shrug. "It's meaningful work and I'm grateful for it."

"Wow." He looks at me with genuine admiration. "You're really something. I admire your conviction. I couldn't do it."

"Well, I couldn't do what you do, either."

"No, you definitely couldn't. It takes a bit more ruthlessness than you have."

I shrug. I'm sure he's right. "So, is it true you have a house in Barbados?"

He laughs. "I've had about ten people suggest we have our next reunion down there. Yes, it's true. You're welcome to visit anytime." He gives me that sexy, lingering gaze again. Then he lowers his eyes and when he looks up, there's no sign of flirtation on his face. "You really don't give a shit that I have a house in Barbados, do you?"

I shake my head. "No. Sorry."

He presses his lips together, his smile sad. "Don't be sorry. It's so damn refreshing. God, it really is good to see you, Gretchen."

Chimes sound, those charming Country Club chimes, indicating that dinner's about to be served. We both tense, realizing we need to end this private rendezvous. Then Brad's hand skates down my arm, his fingers lightly brushing my fingers. It's the first truly sensual touch I've known in years, and my skin tingles in response. We face each other, our lips only inches apart, our eyes open, waiting to see if the other will make a move.

His phone vibrates again. Glancing at the text, a flicker of concern passes over his face, but he shoves the phone back in his pocket. "It can wait," he says. Then he turns on his sexy bedroom eyes and murmurs, "To be continued?"

I nod and smile. The moment passes. I make myself stand up. He stands too, drapes his arm around my shoulder again, and side by side, we stroll back toward the veranda.

"Are you sitting with anyone for dinner?"

"Yes. Queenie and her friends. There might be room at the table."

"Nah, my football buddies are saving me a seat. A bunch of us are going to the Tavern later tonight. You should come."

"That sounds like fun. I might." I let my hand slide down his hip, just brushing his bottom as I let go.

He leans into me so close that his lips brush my ears. "I'll be seeing you, Gretchen," he whispers, his voice a sensuous promise. Then Brad Atkinson gives my shoulder one last squeeze and heads toward a crowd of large men hailing him from across the room.

4

LAB PARTNERS 4-EVER

I make my way through the crowds, greeting old friends here and there, until I find the circular table for eight where Queenie and her friends sit. Silverware gleams against the white tablecloths, framing plated salads at each place setting. Gentle light and balmy air stream in through the tall open windows and the scent of warm bread in baskets and dishes of garlic butter makes my stomach growl. We settle in, spreading white cloth napkins on our laps, and welcome three other alums looking for spaces until only the seat to my left remains open.

"Mind if I join you?"

The voice is familiar. I glance up to find a man a couple inches taller than myself, slender build, slightly receding hair. My mouth drops open. I stare, not believing my eyes.

"Vic?" I whisper.

He holds my gaze, a small, uncertain smile on his face as he watches for my reaction.

"Hello, Gretchen," he says.

He's much older than the friend I remember from high school. Twenty-six years older, to be precise, almost exactly, since that day in July 1996 when we took water tubes down

Holland Creek, had a bonfire at Lena's house, and I'd introduced Joe to all my high school friends. He's changed, very changed from the dark-haired, fresh-faced, hazel-eyed twenty-two-year-old I'd last seen. He's wearing an olive button-up short-sleeved shirt, khaki pants, and those familiar Clark Kent glasses. Even with his thinning hair and furrowed brow, he's aged into someone strikingly handsome. There's a quiet confidence in him. He eyes me warily.

I know I'm staring at him like an idiot, but I can't believe he's here. I can't believe he's talking to me.

"You weren't... you weren't signed up," I manage to say. "I looked for your name. I looked to see if you were coming. You weren't on the list. You never come to reunions. I was sure you wouldn't be here."

At my words, his posture relaxes just slightly. He shrugs and smiles, his hazel eyes crinkling at the corners just like they used to. "Well, I'm here now," he says. "Do you mind if I join you?"

"Sit down, Vic," say Eva and Lori at the same time.

"Glad you finally made it to one of these," Queenie scolds. "It's about time. We've missed you, you know? What the hell made you stay away for so long?"

Vic smiles at Queenie without responding to her question. He looks around the table, greeting everyone by name without looking at their name tags, and sits down beside me. He must have really studied the yearbook to be able to do that. Or maybe not. Vic has always been attuned to people. Maybe he really does remember everyone, even after all these years. People certainly seem happy to see him if the beaming smiles around the table give any indication.

I stare at him, not smiling. "But you didn't sign up," I say again, seemingly unable to move past this simple fact. "I checked."

"Record, meet Broken," says Queenie.

Lori and Eva giggle, but I can't make myself smile. Vic's presence has thoroughly unsettled me. I hate being unprepared for anything and right now, I am unprepared for Vic to arrive at my table after being utterly absent from my life for twenty-six years and ask if he can join me. Why is he even speaking to me? How in the world is it possible that he is right now sitting beside me, spreading his cloth napkin on his lap, and reaching for his water glass?

"You didn't sign up till the last minute, either," he murmurs.

"How do you know?"

"Because I checked the list. Just like you did." He gives me a cautious smile.

"Well, I'm always the last one to sign up officially, but everyone on Facebook knew I was coming."

"I believe I was the last one to sign up 'officially' this time. And I'm not on Facebook."

"I know you're not," I snap. "You should join. It's a great way to keep up with everyone. At least it is for people who care about keeping up with their friends. And then I would have known...." I shake my head with frustration.

A server comes around offering bottles of red and white wine.

"Do you have iced tea?" Vic asks.

The man shakes his head. "Sparkling water."

"I'll have that," Vic says. "You?" he asks me.

"Red, please." Do I ever need a glass of wine.

The server pours my merlot and motions over a teenage boy carrying seltzer water. When our glasses are filled, I turn to him. "Oh, Vic, I'm sorry. I don't mean to be rude. You've just surprised me. What made you decide to come after all these years?" *Why did you ghost me?* I want to add, but the thought makes it as far as my throat and I swallow it down.

He smiles, his lips closed, his hazel eyes lingering on mine, tilting his head to the side, the gesture so familiar, giving the impression he's thinking of something amusing. I can't believe he's here. I can't believe our thighs are almost touching, our arms brushing against each other, the chairs being crammed together so closely. When had I last been this close to him? When we were lab partners? Prom night? I can't believe he's talking to me, like there hasn't been a decades-long rift between us. We both pick up our glasses, look at each other with cautious eyes, and clink our glasses together. He leaves my question hanging in the air, unanswered, and digs into his salad.

I sip my wine, then turn away, focusing my eyes on the peony centerpiece, trying to make myself take deep breaths. It's not easy. My heart pounds, my emotions swirl around in my gut, this way and that. If I can come out of this weekend being friends with Vic again, that might be the best thing to happen to me this entire decade. But I'm going to have to work to keep my tone free of accusation and blame. He's not stupid. He must have some idea how much his disappearance from my life hurt me. No response when I invited him to my wedding. No Christmas cards in response to mine. My emails to him going into a black hole somewhere. His parents, who used to like me so much, greeting me stiffly at the door, not inviting me in, telling me they'd make sure Vic got the message that I'd stopped by. It took me a while, but I got his message, too. It's been over twenty years since I'd made any efforts to connect. He decided he didn't want me in his life, and I accepted it.

So, what is he doing here now?

Suddenly, a new feeling overpowers both hope and hurt. Rage. Who treats a friend the way he treated me? Why am I letting him sit here and talk to me as if we have some kind of friendship when we don't?

I close my eyes and force all my feelings down. I have no idea what's happening right now, but one thing I know: I need to behave like a functional adult at a thirtieth high school reunion and, if nothing else, be polite. But let him carry the conversational ball uphill. I'll answer his questions in a civil manner. I don't need to offer anything more. As far as I'm concerned, Vic will have to be satisfied with monosyllables out of me. That's all he deserves.

A server comes by to take our meal orders: salmon, chicken, or pasta primavera. I order the pasta primavera and Vic orders poached salmon.

"It's been a long time," Vic says, his voice quiet. "I was afraid you wouldn't remember me. I'm glad you do."

Forgetting all my resolve, I turn to him with quiet fury. "You did not for one minute worry that I wouldn't remember you, Vic Abernathy."

He freezes, holding his water glass in the air, watching my face, his own face a studied calm. "A little," he says.

"No."

He glances down at his plate, exhaling slowly, then faces me again, biting back a smile. "You're right. I didn't. You haven't changed."

"Of course I have," I snap.

"Nope," Queenie says, butting into our conversation with the calm authority of a woman much experienced in conflict management. "Vic's right. You look exactly the same." Lori and Eva nod. "It's a compliment, girl. Take it."

"I wasn't talking about her looks." Vic glances my way again, giving me a cursory up-and-down scan. "There's nothing wrong with your looks. Don't get me wrong."

Nothing wrong with my looks? He's teasing me! He doesn't have the right to tease me this way, just like he used to. In high school, I often asked him how I looked, blatantly fishing for compliments and he'd say, "not terrible," or "there's nothing wrong with the way you look," but there would always be some twinkle in his eyes that let me know he liked what he saw. In my moments of deepest teenage insecurity, he made me feel better.

Vic likes what he sees now. I can tell. Especially when he catches my eye again, half-smiles, and turns away. I want to laugh, and I want to cry.

"Vic," I whisper.

"Gretchen," he says. "You should eat your salad before they take it away. If things are still run the way they were when I waited on tables here, there's a strict schedule and they'll be snatching that plate away in about—" he glances at his watch— "four minutes."

I still can't smile. "I never expected to see you again," I say. "Given that you dropped off the face of the earth."

He swallows, his eyes on his plate, before giving me a side glance. "I'm sorry," he murmurs.

For what? What exactly are you sorry for, Vic? I want to holler at him, but I breathe in deeply and take a bite of my salad. "I don't know anything about your life. Well, other than that your mother died a few years ago. My parents told me that. I'm sorry for your loss."

He gives me an odd look. "Thanks," he says.

"And I know you're married. Your wife didn't want to come?"

I feel Queenie's eyes on me and glance up to see her shaking her head in surprise. Is there something I'm supposed to know? Something Queenie knows and I don't? Is he divorced, too? I turn back to Vic. He's staring at his plate.

"My wife died, too," he says.

Oh, my God. His wife died? How was I supposed to know that? It's his fault I don't know anything about his life. How does Queenie know this, and I don't? She looks shocked, too. Does she not realize that Vic and I lost touch? Did he keep up with her, but not with me? I'm hurt and embarrassed and furious.

Then I crumple inside. What right do I have to be angry with him? His wife died.

"I'm sorry, Vic. I'm really sorry for your loss," I say for the second time in two minutes.

"Thank you," he repeats and turns back to his salad.

I twist my napkin. I have so many emotions flying around inside me, I can't think straight.

"What was her name?" I ask. *And why didn't you invite me to your wedding, like I invited you to mine? Maybe I'd have refused to respond and then you would have a taste of what that felt like.* I glance at his left hand. He's taken off his wedding ring.

"Her name was Hong Li," he says. "You would have liked her."

"Of course I would have," I say. "I would have liked any woman smart enough to marry you." *But I never had a chance to meet her, did I?* I chase a crouton around my salad plate till my fork accidentally catapults it into the breadbasket. "Oops." I glance at him. My cheeks heat when I see him biting back a smile. I was somewhat notorious in high school for messing up in little ways in science class, usually because I wasn't paying enough attention and skipped steps in experiments or forgot to start the timer when that was my only job. Though there was also the time I accidentally cut the frog we were dissecting almost in half because I couldn't bear to look at what I was doing and then I was so upset at what I'd done that I fainted. I don't know how he put up with me as his lab partner for four years.

"She was sick, wasn't she?" Queenie says. When he looks up, apparently surprised that she knows this, she adds, "You know your dad and my dad still play poker together, right?"

"Right," he says, smiling. "I did know that. Yeah. She was sick. Motor neuron disease. It was brutal, but she was incredibly strong." His salad plate empty, he puts down his fork and rubs his hands on his thighs. Another gesture that seems shockingly familiar, though it's been decades since I'd seen it. "It's been three years."

I wonder if Vic is going to want to talk to the woman on the other side of him, but although he smiles at her graciously several times, he keeps his focus on me. Despite my previous determination not to make conversation with him, I find myself doing just that.

"So, you became a chemistry teacher?"

He nods. "I did. In a science magnet high school."

"That's funny. I mean, it seems like a strange coincidence," I say. "My husband is a chemistry professor. You met him. Joe."

"Yes." Vic nods. "We met." He glances at my bare left hand. "Husband? I thought I'd heard that...."

"That we divorced?" I ask. "Yes. We divorced." *Why am I still calling Joe my husband?*

"How did that go?"

I shrug. "As divorces go, it's been astonishingly cordial. More than that. Friendly. I mean, the kids still wish we hadn't split up, but once Annie, his current wife, joined the faculty, it was all over between me and Joe. I mean, our marriage was over. But we're still friends. Somehow, he convinced me he still really loved me as a friend, and I believed him. It's strange, I know. In fact, I was just talking to him on my drive here. He asked me if you were coming."

Vic raises his eyebrows at that, though his eyes return to his plate. "Did he?"

"Yes. I think he liked you. I mean, obviously you made an impression on him, since he remembered you after all these years and you only met that one time. Did you like Joe?" I blurt out, then want to kick myself for asking. What does it matter if Vic liked Joe or not?

Vic looks at me, now drumming his hands on his thighs. Is he nervous?

"I'd like any man smart enough to marry you," he says.

We stare at each other for a moment. Then he smiles and I can't keep myself from smiling back or from feeling a flood of relief, of wonder, of joy. I can't believe this. I've never even let myself hope that Vic and I might somehow become friends again. For a moment, I even fear I'm dreaming because I'd had dreams like this. Wish fulfillment dreams. But I'm not dreaming. He's really here.

Eva taps my arm and hands me a cellphone with a screen shot of two adorable girls in flowery sundresses. "Lori's grand-children," she says. "Pass it around."

"They're adorable," I say to Lori. I pass the phone to Vic.

"And here are mine." Eva hands me her phone with a photo of two boys who might be in kindergarten or first grade, dressed in mini tuxedos.

"What was the occasion?" I ask.

"The photo shoot," Eva says, challenging me to make some comment about that choice of attire, but of course, I wouldn't dare. I pass this phone on to Vic, too, and Eva hands me another phone, Queenie's, with a photo of her daughter holding an infant. "Six weeks old," Queenie says proudly.

"None of you look like you could be grandmothers," I say, internally reeling. I try to do the math in my head and give up. In no universe am I ready to be a grandmother. I pass Queenie's phone to Vic.

"Cute," Vic says, and passes the phone to his neighbor.

We all lean back in our chairs as servers remove our salad plates, mine practically untouched, and place our main courses in front of us. Vic called that right: there's a very efficient serving operation happening in this place.

"Oh, my God!" Across the table, Lori half stands and claps

her hands together. "I just realized something. You two are the Lab Partners! I was looking through our yearbook this morning and there was the cutest picture of the two of you in a chemistry lab, wearing white coats and goggles. The caption said, 'Lab Partners 4-Ever.' I was sorry to hear about your wife, Vic. And I'm so glad you finally came back to a reunion."

Vic doesn't look at me, and I don't look at him.

"Thank you," he says to Lori.

"Did you have children?" she asks.

I glance at him. More information I don't have.

"I have a daughter. She's seventeen. Staying with friends this weekend." He returns my gaze. "You have children, don't you?"

"A son and a daughter in their early twenties." I want to see a photo of his daughter. And his wife, too. I pull out my phone and pull up a recent picture of Alistair and Fiona taken in front of blue hydrangeas in Fort Tryon Park. "Here they are," I say. "Do you have any pictures of Hong Li... and what is your daughter's name?"

"Caroline." He seems momentarily reluctant, but then he pulls out his phone and shows me a photo of an elegant, very thin Asian woman in a wheelchair, a teenage girl with long brown hair squatting on one side of the chair, and Vic squatting on the other. They're all smiling. Looking happy.

"What a lovely family," I murmur.

He nods and puts his phone away.

"I'm really sorry for your loss, Vic," I say, yet again. "Such an awful thing to go through."

He looks at me. "It was awful. I miss her. But life has a way of going on. It's been wonderful being a father. It's gone fast, though."

"I know. I really miss it. Well," I amend, "Except for the years between twelve and sixteen, especially for my daughter. Those years went by at a glacial pace. Fiona seemed to believe that everything wrong in the entire universe was my fault. Was it the same with Caroline?"

Vic smiles hesitantly, then says, "It hasn't been easy with Caroline, especially since...." He shrugs. "She misses her mother. Of course. But the last year has gotten better."

"They grow up," I say. "Thank God." I laugh and raise my wineglass. He raises his seltzer. We clink again and drink. "So, how do you like Seattle?"

"I like it. It's a great city. Of course, it has its problems, like every place does."

"Such as?"

"There's an issue with affordable housing, for one. Lots of people without homes, living on the street. Mental health issues."

"Plus, poverty," says Queenie, butting in. "Plus, eviction. Lots of reasons people end up living on the streets, not just mental illness."

"True," says Vic.

"It's like this country doesn't think people have the inalienable right to a safe place to live," I say.

Vic watches as I accept another glass of wine from a passing server. I've never been much of a drinker, which I'm sure he remembers, but I need some liquid courage to deal with his presence. "Seattle has some innovative strategies for addressing these problems," Vic says.

"Really?" I want to press him, genuinely curious to learn more about what Seattle is doing to tackle the issues that consume my working life.

"Really." He smiles, and I suspect Vic knows exactly what I do professionally, that he raised the topic because he knew I'd be interested. Which also means he must have asked someone about me, and that warms my heart.

Then a flicker of emotion—I can't name it—uncertainty?

guilt? resignation?—flashes across Vic's face as he lowers his glass. A moment later, I sense a presence behind my chair. I look up to find Brad standing there, hands on his hips, grinning at Vic.

"No way, man," Brad says, shaking his head. "No way."

Smiling sheepishly, Vic pushes back his chair and stands. Brad embraces him in a bear hug.

"Where the hell have you been?" Brad pushes Vic away so he can take him to task. "That was some disappearing act, Houdini. I wondered if you'd died. How many emails did I send you about this reunion? Ten? You think you could have responded to a single one?"

"I'm sorry," Vic says. "I appreciated you reaching out. I didn't get back to you because I wasn't sure about my plans. But I'm here."

"You are the last person from high school I expected to disappear on us. It's been years, man." Brad turns to me. "Did you know he was coming?"

I shake my head.

"But you two must have kept up," Brad says.

"Nope," I say. "He didn't respond to any of my emails, either."

"You tried to get him to come back this year, too?"

"Nope," I say again. "I gave up trying to get any response from him twenty years ago." I turn to my dinner and shove a big forkful of penne in my mouth to keep myself from saying anything more.

"Uh oh." Brad laughs, raising an eyebrow at Vic. "Someone's in the doghouse. Gretchen, you don't mind if I borrow Vic for a little while, do you? There are two tables of football players who insisted my eyes were playing tricks on me when I told them our statistician finally decided to make an appearance. Come on, buddy. You've got some explaining to do." Brad loops an arm around Vic's shoulder and drags him away. I follow their trek through the room, unable to keep my eyes off Vic, fearful that if I do, he might vanish again. Every step he takes, it seems someone jumps up to give him a hug or a high five. I'm not the only one who's missed him, obviously.

I try to force another bite of pasta, but I can't. My appetite has vanished. I stand up. "Sorry, ladies. I need a breather. I'm just going to step outside for a few minutes."

"Need company?" Queenie asks.

"No. I need to be by myself. But I'll be back. I don't believe in disappearing on people without a word. Or not responding when people reach out to you over and over again. I don't think it's right to...."

"Gretchen," Queenie interrupts. "No need to explain, honey. Go take your breather."

I fling my cloth napkin onto my chair and make my way to an exit in the back of the room, not wanting to make my departure obvious, then hurry to the copse of trees that Brad and I had walked to earlier. Relieved I didn't pass anyone on the way, I plop down on the bench, hidden from view from the veranda, cross my arms over my chest, and tilt my head back. Stars twinkle faintly in the sky, which has turned a dusky gray. Gradually, the sky grows darker, blacker. The stars brighten and multiply. I sit there, my mind curiously empty, my eyes on the sky.

Finally, I shake myself, stand up, and head back toward the clubhouse. The sound of cars driving out of the parking lot surprises me. How long have I been gone? I hurry onto the veranda and step through the clubhouse doors to find the room nearly two-thirds empty. I weave in between tables, making my way back to my seat. The dinner plates have been removed, desserts left in their place, and half the chairs at the table are vacant. Only Queenie, Lori, and Eva remain seated, spooning up heavenly looking chocolate mousse from sundae glasses, pointedly not looking at me. An untouched dish of chocolate mousse topped with a mound of whipped cream and a mint leaf graces my place setting. I sit down, glancing at the empty seat to my left, then look about the room, trying to spot Vic.

"He left," Queenie says.

I catch her eye. She shakes her head, eyeing me with amusement, then slides another spoonful of mousse into her mouth, closing her eyes to savor the taste. I pick up my spoon, pull out the little mint leaf from the whipped cream, and do the same. When all four of us have devoured every last dollop of chocolate mousse, I sit back in my chair and glance back and forth between the three women, who remain silent.

"What?" I finally demand.

Queenie rests her elbows on the table and her chin on her folded hands. "I don't know, girl. Just wondering if history's repeating itself. The same two guys after the same one girl. Only question is if the woman that girl grew into has gotten any smarter after all these years."

"Vic was never after me," I correct her. "We were just friends. That's all he wanted. He made that absolutely clear to me in high school. And I was committed to our friendship, and he dropped me, with no explanation. I don't owe him anything. And Brad, for your information, was never really after me, either, but he's always stayed in touch with me. I get a Christmas card from him every year. And he comments on my Facebook posts."

"Honestly, Gretchen, you don't think that man sends his own Christmas cards, do you?" Lori says. "Everyone in our class gets a Christmas card from Brad."

I'm about to insist that of course he sends his own cards when I recall that there haven't been any personal notes in his cards for many years now. "Well, who cares? Brad was in touch with me before this reunion. I knew he was going to be here, and I knew he was looking forward to seeing me. Vic showed up like a... like a ghost." I shake my head, disbelieving. And now he's gone without saying goodbye, and I'm probably never going to see him again. Suddenly, I have a fervent wish that I hadn't seen him tonight, or talked to him, or clinked glasses with him. This brief time together has brought back everything I lost when he cut off our friendship. "And then he disappeared on me. Again," I whisper.

I close my eyes. It's been a long, long time since I cried over Vic and I'd been absolutely private about it when I had, never wanting to give Joe the impression that I had intense feelings for another man, which he might have misinterpreted. Even though Vic and I were just friends. Had been just friends. I grit my teeth.

I'm sure as hell not going to cry over Vic now.

Queenie clears her throat to get my attention. "Just a minor point of clarification," she says. "From Vic's perspective, it's possible it seemed like you were the one who disappeared tonight." She raises her eyebrow at me. "Anyway, I promised I'd pass along a message to you."

I lean forward, gripping the table's edge with my hands. Vic left a message for me? "What did he say?"

"He said he's taking the tour of the school tomorrow at 10:30. He's interested in seeing the new science labs, apparently."

"Oh." I let out a slow exhale. This is the first message Vic has left for me in decades. I look around the table. "Well, of course I want to see what the new science labs look like, too. Don't you all?"

All three of them shake their heads. "We live here," Eva says. "We've seen them."

"And Brad said to remind you he'll be at the Tavern later tonight and you better keep your promise and meet him there," Lori says. She glances at Queenie and Eva. "Did any other men leave messages for Gretchen?" The other two women shake their heads.

I smile, feeling sheepish. "Well, thank you for waiting. I appreciate it."

"We weren't going to let them take away your chocolate mousse, given that you hardly had a bite of dinner and knowing how much we all paid for this meal."

"I appreciate that," I say. "And Queenie, you're wrong about Vic being after me."

"Girlfriend." Queenie returns to her previous posture, elbows on the table, chin resting on her intertwined fingers, and challenges me with her uncompromising gaze. "I am never wrong."

"Well, you're wrong this time," I insist.

She shrugs. "I suppose there's a first time for everything. So, maybe it didn't bother Vic when the football players all teased Brad about your little private time together behind the fir trees before dinner," she adds.

I stare at her, feeling strangely uneasy to hear this. But she's still wrong. I toss my cloth napkin onto the table, push back my chair, and stand with my hands on my hips. "How would you have any idea what boys might have been interested in me in high school?" I press. "We weren't even friends back then."

"I wasn't friends with you," she says with a shrug. "But I was friends with Vic. And am I surprised you didn't know that? No, I am not. You always had your head in the clouds, and I mean that in the nicest possible way. And on that note, ladies, this grandmother is going to call it a night. My daughter is probably at her wits' end with a colicky baby. I'm the only one who can calm that darling down."

"Queenie," I say, as the four of us weave our way through the tables and empty chairs to the front door. "I need to know. Did Vic keep up with you?"

She shrugs. "For a few years. And I saw him at his mother's funeral, of course, but that was the last time. I was hurt, at first, when he stopped responding to my texts, but once I heard his wife was sick, I didn't take it personally." She smiles at me. "He's here now, and he's Vic, you know. We all loved him. And so, we welcome him back with open arms."

"That's the royal we, Queenie?" Lori asks, elbowing Eva.

The two women burst into giggles, but Queenie merely nods. Though shorter than us all, she holds her head high, and with a stately air, leads our group out of the club and toward the parking lot.

5

ROCK LOBSTERS AND BUNSEN BURNERS

The Village Café still makes the best Belgian waffles. I push back my plate, unable to eat the last syrup-drenched bite. "I'm so full. And it was so worth it," I say.

"We'll work it off on our hiking weekend in August," Lena says, sipping her latte.

Sophia nods, closing her eyes and smiling in pleasure. Then she opens them, gazing around the bustling café with disapproval. "I'm so sorry they renovated this place. I miss the booths."

"Sophia, there were termites in those booths," Anne-Marie says, scrunching her nose. "They were from the Middle Ages, honestly."

We used to be able to find "Rock Lobsters" and all our initials carved in the fourth booth, but yellow wallpaper with daisies has replaced the dark wall panels, while small tables with red and white checkered cloths occupy the booths' old territory. The atmosphere is cheery and fresh, as opposed to cozy and dingy. I miss the old booths, too, but I don't mind the changes, and it certainly seems good for business, given the crowd. Everything needs a makeover from time to time.

"So, what happened last night?" Lena says. "Everyone expected you to come to the Tavern. Brad kept asking when you'd be there."

"Where'd you go, anyway?" Anne-Marie says. "We looked all over the club but couldn't find you anywhere."

"But your car was still in the parking lot," Sophia adds.

I shrug. "I got a little overwhelmed seeing everyone again, honestly. So, I just went out on the golf course for some quiet time. And then I went home and talked to my parents. A typical exciting Friday night in Warren." I sip my coffee and smile.

"It was," says Lena. "You just missed the excitement. The Tavern was hopping."

I haven't mentioned Vic all morning and neither have they. They were all friends with him, too, and hurt when he dropped out of our lives, but at my earnest request, we all agreed years ago to stop speculating about why and they promised to never mention his name again unless I brought him up first. They're sticking to that promise, but they keep giving each other knowing glances. Everyone at the reunion saw us sitting together last night and talking. My friends are no exception. But I don't say anything because I don't know what to say. I'm afraid of getting enraged. I'm afraid of crying. I'm afraid to hope for anything.

My phone dings with a calendar reminder and I jump. "Oops, I forgot about the school tour," I say, reaching for my wallet to pull out some cash. "It starts at 10:30. Are you all coming to that?"

They all glance at each other, biting back smiles.

Lena says, "We can't. We're all going to Sophia's to set up for the pool party this afternoon. Did you forget you signed up for that, too?"

My eyes widen in consternation. I completely forgot I'd volunteered to do set-up.

"Since when are you interested in seeing renovated high school chemistry labs, anyway?" Anne-Marie says. "Given he who shall not be named, meaning..." she clears her throat and glances at Lena, who's rolling her eyes right on cue, "Joe, just to be clear, I would think you'd have had your fill of all things chemistry."

"I'm just really interested in seeing what they've done," I say. "Seriously, none of you want to come?"

"I can't stand change," Sophia says. "I don't want to see a shiny new auditorium. I want to remember our decrepit old theater where I sang `I Cain't Say No.' My one moment of stardom."

"Well, I am not clinging to the past," I say, standing up. "And I'm interested in the tour. Please tell me you'll be fine setting up for the pool party without me."

They all remain seated and look up at me, waiting patiently.

I put my hands on my hips and stare them down. "What do you want me to say?" I demand.

"Lab partners '4-Ever'?" Lena asks, putting air quotes over the '4-Ever' we'd written on our chemistry class binders.

I throw up my hands and sigh. "I don't know what to tell you," I say. "He came back. I don't know why. But you, more than anyone, know how important his friendship was to me and how hurt I was when he vanished from my life. I never wanted to lose touch with him. So, he traveled 3000 miles to be here this weekend and I'm going to be the friend to him that I always expected him to be to me. Anyway, I'm not a hundred percent sure he'll be there."

"Oh, he'll be there," Lena says. "He was at the Tavern last night and he made sure we all knew that he'd be going on the tour today. He wanted to make sure you got that message."

A deeply wounded place in my heart tingles and warms, as if beginning to heal.

"Okay, so we'll cover for you setting up for the party and you take the tour and make sure to give us a full report on all the school's capital improvements, especially the chemistry labs," Anne-Marie says, a business-like expression on her face. "We want to know the total budget, how many new Bunsen burners there are, the model of the safety goggles, and whether it follows the CDC's School Chemistry Lab Safety Guidelines."

I stare at her with confusion. Her straight face breaks into a laugh. "Just have fun," she says. "I hope the tour is everything you want it to be."

They stand to give me hugs.

"You all caught up with him last night?" I ask. They nod. "Why didn't you say anything? Do you have any idea why he came back?"

They glance at each other, their faces all innocence, and shrug and shake their heads.

"No idea," Lena says.

"None," Sophia says.

"It was a rock," Anne-Marie whispers.

"Rock Lobster!" we all whisper back. In high school, we used to shout it, but now we try not to be annoying.

I hug my friends close. "I love you guys."

I leave the café and take the shortcut that slopes downhill behind the row of shops. I pass the bank on my right and the grocery store on my left, cross the street and arrive in the courtyard between the middle school and the high school at 10:30AM on the dot. A couple dozen classmates have gathered by the flagpole, including Vic and Brad, who are joking with each other, seeming on excellent terms. They both smile when they see me approach, but only Brad steps forward, gathering me in a side hug and squeezing my shoulder.

"There she is," he says. "Now we can start the tour."

Vic shoves his hands in his pockets and turns away, focusing his attention on the tour guide, a woman who doesn't look a day over thirty-five, who identifies herself as Ms. Alice Jennings, the high school principal. She wears a form-fitting ivory suit with open-toed, red, high-heeled pumps she seems to have no trouble striding around in. I expect Ms. Jennings would be comfortable on a fashion runway or a movie set, but I would turn an ankle trying to walk in shoes like that.

I worry Vic might keep his distance from me after Brad's embrace, so I'm determined not to be in lockstep with Brad. Brad makes this easy by abandoning me completely in favor of the glamorous principal and as we make our way into the high school, Vic walks beside me. I expected to be anxious, but instead, I'm struck by how familiar and natural it feels to be walking next to him. He makes easy conversation with others around us, seeming surprised and pleased by how glad people are to see him again.

"You had a lot of friends here," I murmur when we pause in the hallway and there's a lull in conversation.

"Yeah." He holds my gaze.

I've forgotten how much I liked his eyes. I used to think the Clark Kent glasses were adorably nerdy, but fashion trends have caught up with him, it seems. Now they look hot. He's aged well. Very well.

"I'm glad I came back." Vic eyes me quizzically. "What are you thinking?"

"Silver fox," I say.

His hazel eyes widen.

I clap a hand over my mouth and turn away from him, shaking my head and walking after the group. "Sorry," I say over my shoulder, hoping I'm not about to blush. "I have this awful habit of blurting out embarrassing things." I stop when I realize Vic isn't beside me and turn around.

He's standing motionless in the hallway a few feet away, his hands in his pockets, staring at me. Then he burst out laughing. "Yes," he says. "I remember."

We spend the next hour peeking into air-conditioned classrooms where summer school is in session (no air conditioning existed when we went to school here), and then moving on to tour the upgraded athletic fields and science wing, everything shiny, clean, professional looking.

"I can barely recognize this as our old school," I say to murmurs of agreement.

"We've had some very generous donors." Ms. Jennings gives a shy side-glance at Brad, who eyes the floor modestly, then tilts his head up and winks at her. God, I know that wink. And I expect I also know exactly how hard Ms. Jennings' heart is fluttering right now. And yet, I'm not feeling jealous at all. I'm enjoying seeing Brad, but my desire for any kind of fling with him this weekend has dissipated overnight.

"Good to know some things never change," I whisper to Vic, who grins.

Brad glances at us as if sensing that he's the topic of conversation and he smiles as if certain he'd appreciate whatever we're saying. When a student comes up to the principal, pulling her away for a moment, Brad confidently takes over the tour. Apparently, this isn't his first time seeing the improvements.

"Hey, Vic," he says. "You're going to like this, buddy."

We follow him down the hall to the new chemistry lab. It's a sight to see, glowing white tables, long white counters along the walls with shiny built-in sinks every few paces, shelves of safety equipment, measuring tools, test tubes, funnels, bottles, beakers, flasks, everything looking orderly and spotless. Brad keeps his eyes on Vic, waiting for his reaction.

Vic looks around the room appreciatively, then clears his throat. "Impressive. Hey, I know a high school in Seattle that could use some upgrades, too. I guess I should explore their alumni support network, see if we have any deep pockets there. I gather this new wing might be the Atkinson wing?"

"Knock it off." Brad punches Vic lightly on the shoulder, though he doesn't seem to mind the inquiry. "You know I don't care about that kind of thing. But about your school, let's talk later."

"I'm joking, Brad," Vic says.

"I'm not." Brad places a heavy hand on Vic's shoulder.

"Hey," says a balding, heavyset classmate I don't recognize at all. "Vic! Gretchen! You two need to put on some goggles. We've got to get a 'then and now' photo for our Facebook page."

Seeming grateful for the interruption, Vic eases away from Brad and grabs a couple pairs of goggles off a shelf. We put them on and pose on either side of a Bunsen burner.

Then Ms. Jennings returns, and Brad assumes his place at her side. The principal leads the way down a long, clean hall with empty classrooms and gleaming lockers. I find it hard to believe any kids attend this school, though I saw proof earlier. It all looks so pristine. I glance at Vic to see if he has a similar reaction.

He shrugs. "My school doesn't look like this," he whispers.

"Last but not least," Ms. Jennings says, "The new theater and auditorium." She opens a double door and leads us into an elegant hall with plush red seats, a wide stage, and what looks like professional lighting equipment above the balcony. "Not to repeat myself," she says, "but I can't emphasize enough what a difference alumni support for the school can make for the current student body. And I have some exciting news to share that I know your class will appreciate. The school board voted at last week's meeting to name our new auditorium Atkinson Hall, after one of our most distinguished alumni." She beams at Brad, her cheeks flushing. We all clap, and several people whistle.

Brad stands with his mouth open and eyes wide, appearing genuinely surprised.

"I loved this place, Alice," he says modestly. "These old stomping grounds made me what I am. The least I can do is give back, given how fortunate I've been."

Back in the courtyard, we part from the principal and people peel off, saying, "See you at the pool party." Then somehow, only Brad, Vic, and I remain. The two of them glance at each other and at me. I have the strangest sense of déjà vu.

Was Queenie right? Had it been like this in high school, the two of them competing for me? No. In high school and when we were home from college, Brad had one girlfriend after another. I was his in-between fling. And Vic had never competed for me. He didn't want to. We were close friends, which was all he wanted. Right? Didn't he make that absolutely clear to me on prom night, the one time I wondered if we might be more than friends? We spent loads of time together in high school and on our college breaks, but there was never any question in his mind of the two of us going out. Was there?

Oh, I have no idea! All I know for certain is that right now, I'm standing in between the only two men besides my ex-husband that I've ever had fervent feelings for and neither one of them is budging. This is not turning out to be the weekend I'd expected.

"Well, Vic," Brad says, "Great catching up with you, man. See you at the pool party? Gretchen, I was thinking we could take a walk today, down that path by the creek, for old time's sake." He smiles his full-wattage smile and holds out a hand as if he has no doubt, none at all, that I will go for a "walk" with him now.

With apology in my eyes, I shake my head. "Brad, I'm sorry. Vic and I haven't seen each other for a long time, and we didn't really have a chance to talk much last night. And we have a lot to talk about. Don't we, Vic?" I can't keep the sharp edge out of my voice.

Vic nods, his expression solemn.

Brad looks back and forth between us, as if assessing us in a new way. "Oh," he says. "Okay then." He studies Vic for a moment. "Man, I thought if you were going to keep up with anyone it would have been Gretchen, but... you didn't?" Vic shrugs and turns away. Brad winks at me, this time not flirtatious at all. "I'll see you kids later," he says.

I watch him walk away with his characteristic swagger, heading back into the school. It must be nice to go through life so sure of yourself, I think. Then I remember the loneliness I sensed in him when we were together last night behind the fir trees. There are chinks in that Atkinson armor, and knowing that makes me warm to him even more.

6

PIECE OF MIND

Vic stands, his arms hanging loosely at his sides, facing away from me. I cross my arms, hug my ribs, and move to his side. Neither of us smiles.

"Playground?" he asks.

I fall into step beside him. We walk across the high school baseball diamond, past the tennis courts, and down a gently sloping hill until we arrive at our old haunting ground at the back of the elementary school. When we were in high school, we used to come here late at night to sit on the swings and talk. His parents didn't want him to go to college, much less go into teaching. They wanted him to stay in town and take over the family business. My parents also wanted to keep me local, and wanted me to go into teaching, not social work. We both hated disappointing our parents, but we longed to leave the safety and familiarity of our hometown and experience city life somewhere.

How many hopes and dreams had we shared with each other while sitting on those swings?

The playground, too, has undergone refurbishments. Gone

are the wooden teeter-totters, the faded merry-go-round, the steep metal slides, the tall monkey bars, the metal jungle gyms—all deemed health hazards in this new era. A bright blue, rubbery surface has replaced the grass and dirt. New climbers, slides, swings, tunnels, bridges, stairways, ramps, ladders come in vibrant reds and yellows and greens, all solid, smooth, splinter-free plastic. As a parent who has raised young children in playgrounds like this in New York City, I appreciate how safe and controlled the environment seems. As a nostalgic adult, I miss those burning hot slides, the monkey bars from which I'd fallen and broken my arm, the splintery teeter-totters, the wobbly merry-go-round.

We make our way to the older kids' swing set, choose adjacent swings, and sway side by side, dragging our shoes on the plastic turf. "I miss the dirt," I say. Then I laugh at a memory. "You and Brad used to push me on the old merry-go-round. Remember? Third or fourth grade, I think?"

Vic nods, smiling. "Yes. We would race each other out after lunch to see who could get there first for the privilege of pushing you on that thing fast enough to make you laugh. And see your hair blow wild in the breeze."

Was that a romantic thing to say? It sounds romantic. Did Vic have a crush on me in fourth grade? He'd been such a cute boy. I used to chase him around the town swimming pool every summer before he grew into the lifeguard that scolded the younger kids not to run on the cement. I look him over as subtly as I can. He still appears every bit a swimmer, his shoulders broad, arms strong, abdomen firm.

"You're swimming?" I ask.

He smiles, nodding. "About a mile a day, most days. I stopped for a few years, but after...." He swallows and turns away, blinking his eyes. "After Hong Li died, I started up again. What about you?"

"I make it to the YMCA a couple of times a week. Do you ever come home, Vic?"

He clears his throat. "Home has been Seattle for a long time now."

"Do you ever come home to Warren?"

"I came a couple times a year when Caroline was little. She was eight when Hong Li was diagnosed. After that, my parents came out to see us. Then I came back here to see my mom when she got sick. And then for her funeral. But I haven't been back much."

"Caroline was fourteen when Hong Li died?"

Vic nods, swallowing. "Yes. Too young."

I'm not sure if he's referring to Caroline or Hong Li. Probably both. "I'm so sorry. Did you... did you have a good marriage? I'm not trying to pry, I just... I hoped that for you."

Vic glances at me. His lips press together in a sad smile. "We did. She saved me." He gives a short laugh. "That's sounds overly dramatic. But I was a little lost, and she found me. That's what our marriage felt like. Like I'd been lost and then found. I loved her very much." His voice cracks on the words. He pauses, seeming to need a moment to collect himself. "We met in grad school. She was a fourth-grade teacher. An amazing teacher. On her way to becoming principal when she got her diagnosis."

"That must have been so hard." I twist my swing so I can face him.

"It was. Being sick is fucking expensive on top of everything else."

I smile at this. I remember how surprised people used to be to discover that mild-mannered Vic had a foul mouth.

"I was the sole wage earner," he continues. "The primary caregiver. I became the primary parent, too, though none of us wanted it that way. Caroline was angry. So angry. She's had so much more than her share to deal with."

"Is she still angry?" I ask.

"I think so. I think she just hides it better. She really needs a... well." He shakes his head, not looking at me. "Anyway. It's been hard, but I wouldn't change anything. Having Hong Li in my life for the time I did was a gift. I miss her every day. And I love being a dad, even when my daughter puts me through hell." He glances at me. "Which she does, on occasion."

"I'd like to meet her," I say.

"After that description?" He sways on his swing, turning away from me, then back again. The sun glints off his glasses. "I'd like you to meet her, too," he says. "You wouldn't be able to say you weren't warned." He sighs. "I don't mean that. She's a sweetheart, my daughter. She's just in pain."

We stay silent for a few minutes. Then Vic gives a soft laugh and points his finger. On the other side of the tennis courts, Brad strolls beside Alice Jennings. She's barefoot. They're holding hands. Her red pumps dangle from his other fingers. "Doesn't waste any time, does he?" Vic says.

"No." I smile. "Apparently not."

We watch until they're out of our line of sight.

Then Vic asks, "How was your marriage, Gretchen? Were you and Joe happy, at least for a time?"

"Yes. I thought so, anyway. We had so much fun parenting together. He was a fantastic father. Most of my playground friends were jealous. And he was very supportive of my career. He tolerated me being basically on call all the time and didn't pressure me to get a job that demanded less or paid more. He knew I loved my work. And he liked my friends. He was interested in them. He was so social, much more than I am. He loved coming to these reunions. Can you believe it? Do you know any other spouse who doesn't find it a trying experience?" I close my eyes. "Never mind, you wouldn't have any idea, would you? Unless you went to Hong Li's reunions?" I open my eyes to look at him, and he shakes his head. "Anyway," I continue, "I never enjoyed going to Joe's high school reunions, though I gave it my best effort. He was always interested in my life. So, yes, we were happy. At least, I was. And I thought he was."

I pause, swallowing. The heartache has dulled but not disappeared completely.

"I never dreamed there would be another woman," I whisper. A tear threatens, but I blink it away. "Sorry."

"It's okay," Vic says.

"Joe hated hurting me. That made it better and worse, somehow. It's not like he didn't care about me. Or that he didn't love me anymore. He just didn't want to be married to me anymore. He wanted to be with Annie. I knew her for three years. Saw her at all the faculty parties. And he would talk about her all the time. She was another professor in his department. It never crossed my mind there was anything.... I think Joe was hoping I'd figure it out and confront him. But I didn't. He was so gentle, so sorry, when he told me." I blink rapidly. "I was such a fool, I guess, not to have suspected something. My friends suspected something, but I insisted they were wrong." I sigh. "Oh, well."

"You're trusting," Vic says. "You assume the best in everyone. You look for that. You don't look for anything you're not going to like. You've always been that way. It sounds like he broke your heart."

"Yes." I stare off at the hopscotch design on the edge of the blue mat. "He did. It hurt more than you can imagine."

"Well," Vic says. "I can imagine, actually."

I assume he's talking about Hong Li, though it's not quite the same thing, his wife dying and my husband choosing another woman over me. But who am I to quibble over that? "We managed to salvage a friendship from the wreckage of our marriage, somehow."

I'm tempted to tell Vic how scared I am of being alone for

this next chapter of my life, how much I want to feel loved by someone. I want to tell him how wonderful it feels to be sitting on these swings together, talking to him just like we used to talk, easily, honestly.

It seems like we can talk about everything except what I most want to know: why did Vic break off our friendship with no explanation? And why, after all these years, has he come back to a reunion and sought me out again? We skirt around that topic, circling closer and closer but not landing there.

"I told my dad I'd help him with some repairs around the house this afternoon," Vic finally says. "Are you definitely going to the pool party?"

"I was planning to. I told Sophia and Lena I'd help," I say. "You?"

He nods. "As long as I know you'll be there."

"Vic," I say, gripping the chains of the swing tighter. "You're not going to disappear on me again, are you?"

He lowers his head and rubs his thighs. "No. I'm not. I just need to help my dad right now. I promised."

We get off the swings, face each other awkwardly, then part ways. He heads to his car in the high school parking lot, and I walk back to my parents' house and try to sort out my feelings from all the events of these last twenty-four hours. When I arrive, instead of going inside, I sit on the front porch and pick dead leaves off the potted red geraniums for a few minutes. Then I fish my phone out of my purse and scroll through my contacts. My thumb lingers over Joe's name for a long minute. Then I place the call.

Joe picks up on the second ring. "What's the matter?" he asks, "Is everything okay? Are you having fun? Do your friends still hate me?"

"Yes, I've been having fun. I wouldn't call it hate exactly, but they're not your biggest fans and that's probably not going to change. And I don't know if everything's okay. Joe, I have to ask you something."

"Ask away," he says.

"A few months after we were married, you told me that after the first time I brought you to Warren, you felt like you had to move fast because you thought you had some competition. That there was someone else who was interested in me, someone you thought I might be interested in, too, and you didn't want to risk losing me. Remember?" I'd never asked him who that was because I thought I knew.

"I remember."

"You were talking about Brad, right?"

"Brad?" Joe laughs. "Brad Atkinson? Give me a break, Gretchen. I never felt the slightest competition with Brad. He's not a bad guy, but he's a player, through and through. That little crush you had on him was never going to go anywhere. You never seriously thought it would, did you?"

"Probably not." I put a hand on my stomach, feeling queasy, and close my eyes. "So, who were you talking about?"

He's silent for a long moment. Then he says, "Gretchen, sweetheart, you must know who I was talking about. I was talking about your high school friend who was obviously in love with you. I don't think he felt any real competition from Brad, either. I had a feeling he was waiting for you to pull your head out of the sand about that crush. Maybe. Otherwise, I don't know what the hell he was waiting for. But he knew he had competition from me, all right. And I wasn't going to take any chances, so I made my move."

"Are you talking about Vic?"

"Of course I am," Joe says.

"You only met him that one time. How could you tell all that? We were just friends, Joe. That's all Vic ever wanted from me."

Joe sighs. "Gretchen, you can be a little bit clueless about what's happening right around you. You know that, right? Honestly, it's one of the things I've always loved about you, how determined you are to take things at face value. How accepting you are, how nonjudgmental, how trusting. But it means you sometimes miss something that's staring you in the face."

"Like Annie." Pain twinges at my heart. Joe and I rarely speak about this now.

"Like Annie," Joe says. "I don't know why you were so sure that you and Vic were just friends. It sure as hell wasn't the case for him. I figured that out the first minute I met him. And to be completely honest, I was concerned that it wasn't true for you, either. Feelings as strong as you had for him... those aren't 'just friends' kinds of feelings. I know he really hurt you, cutting you off the way he did. I remember once a Christmas card you sent him came back in the mail and you hid in the bathroom and cried for an hour."

I press a hand to my chest. "Oh, Joe, I'm sorry. I wasn't being secretive. I just never wanted you to think that I had any inappropriate feelings for him."

"I never did think that. I know you thought it was just a strong friendship."

"You think Vic was in love with me?"

"I am one-hundred-percent sure that Vic was in love with you."

"Why didn't you ever tell me?"

Joe gives a short laugh. "I'm telling you now. But why the hell would I have told you then? I didn't want you to love him. I wanted you to love me."

"But if he loved me, why did he drop me so completely?"

"Wait," Joe says. "Wait a minute. Why are you asking me all this? Did Vic show up, after all?"

I sigh. "Yes."

"Is he married?" Joe asks.

"His wife died three years ago."

"Interesting," Joe says.

"Interesting?" I repeat.

"Well, it's sad, of course," Joe says.

"Yes. It's very sad. I wasn't expecting him to be here, but for some reason, he decided to come at the last minute."

"For some reason." I can almost see the exasperated smile on Joe's face. "For some strange reason. Huh. I wonder what that could be."

I sit with my elbows on my knees, cradling my jaw with my palm. "I signed up at the last minute. Like I always do. And then he signed up after me, two days ago."

"Where does he live?" Joe asks.

"Seattle."

"Seattle, huh? That's not exactly around the corner."

"And he has a seventeen-year-old daughter."

"Wow, he had to deal with leaving a seventeen-year-old alone for a weekend. We know how that can work out, don't we?" A moment passes in silence. Then, "Gretchen?" Joe's voice is as gentle as I've ever heard it. "He didn't decide to fly out from Seattle the minute he found out you were coming to the reunion for no particular reason. Go talk to him."

"I have talked to him."

"Go really talk to him. You don't need to wonder about any of this anymore."

I close my eyes, hearing Joe's quiet breathing through the phone. "You were hoping he was going to be here, weren't you?"

"Yeah, I was," Joe says. "I mean, I had no idea if he was married or not, but I hoped maybe he was available. You do hear stories about old sweethearts reconnecting at reunions. I liked him when I met him. And I felt for the guy. I mean, I know what it would have felt like for me if he was the one who got you. I kind of wanted him to have another chance."

"That's so sweet of you to be looking out for Vic that way," I say wryly.

He laughs. "Hey, you know how much I like to look out for Vic."

I press the phone to my ear. My eyes water. Joe still loves me, in his way. He wants me to be happy. To find love again.

"You still there?" Joe asks.

"Yes. Nothing excuses dropping a friend the way Vic dropped me. Nothing."

"So go give him a piece of your mind. Don't hold back. You're magnificent when you're royally pissed off. Gretchen?"

"Yes?"

"Hang up and go."

I say a quick goodbye, put my phone back in my purse, and stand up.

"Gretchen," my father calls from the living room window. "I didn't know you were back."

"Just to get my car," I say. "Vic came to the reunion. I'm going over to his dad's house now to see him." *And give him a piece of my mind.*

"Did he really?" my father says through the screen. "I always liked Vic."

I get in my car and drive five miles out of town to Vic's father's house, a scenic route past farmhouses and silos that I've driven so many times in the past I didn't even have to think about it. I pull up in the driveway of the quaint blue two-story house Vic helped his father build. Vic comes around the side of the house, carrying a ladder. When he sees me, he lowers the ladder to the grass, puts his hands in his pockets, and walks toward my car. The sun glints off his glasses.

"Everything okay?" he asks as I get out.

"No." I slam the door, walk around the car, and lean against the hood, folding my arms across my chest.

He stops a few steps away and waits for me to speak.

"The first time I brought Joe to Warren was the last time you ever talked to me until last night. I was so hurt that you didn't come to my wedding. You didn't even answer the invitation. I sent you Christmas cards for years. I wrote you emails, and you never responded. I called you and you never called back. I came by to see your parents when I was home. I tried everything I could think of to stay in touch with you. You were one of my best friends, Vic."

Tears flood my eyes, despite my best efforts to keep them at bay, and my voice grows husky.

"These are tears of anger, just so you know. I'm so angry at you, Vic. You dumped me. You completely dumped me, and you never told me why. And it really hurt." I fish for tissues in my purse to wipe my eyes. "It was one of the worst things to ever happen to me in my entire life. You should never have treated me that way. I didn't deserve it."

Vic holds my gaze. His brow crinkles, his hazel eyes looking surprised and cautious and sad. "I'm sorry I hurt you, Gretchen. I would never have wanted to hurt you. But I couldn't come to your wedding. I just couldn't. And I couldn't stay friends with you. Not when you married someone else. I'm sorry. I couldn't do it."

"Joe told me you were in love with me." I watch his face.

He turns away from me, looking at the driveway, and gives a short, unsmiling laugh. "Joe told you. When did Joe tell you that?"

"Just now."

He tilts his head back to the sky, his eyes closed, for a long moment. Then he lowers his head and looks at me. "Yeah. I was. For a long time."

"I didn't know that, Vic. You never told me. You never told me!"

"Because you didn't think of me that way."

"That's not true!" I shout, balling my fists, and taking a step in his direction. He stands his ground. "It's not true, Vic. I did think of you that way. I tried to kiss you at prom, and you pushed me away. I wanted you to be my first.... You're the one who made it very clear that in your mind we were just friends."

Vic's eyes widen in surprise. He puts his hands on his hips. "You tried to kiss me because you were trying to make Brad jealous."

"No, I wasn't! I wasn't thinking about Brad. You were the one who was thinking about Brad that night. I was thinking about you. But you made me feel like an absolute fool to think there might be anything more than friendship between us. And I promised myself I was never going to make that mistake again."

Vic stares at me, stroking his jaw with one hand. "Fuck," he whispers. "Really?"

I fold my arms across my chest. "Really. I was so embarrassed, and I was afraid of losing you. That's the one thing I absolutely didn't want to happen. I didn't want to lose you."

He shakes his head. "For the next three years, whenever we came back from college, you were still going off with Brad whenever he crooked his finger your way. And you were constantly talking to me about Brad. You told me he hinted he might propose to you some day, when the fucking stars aligned."

"I thought if you knew I was thinking about Brad, you wouldn't worry that I was thinking about you. Were you really worried about Brad and me?"

Vic shakes his head again. "No. I mean, it sure as hell wasn't fun to see you fawning over him, but I knew you were too smart to end up with him, and I trusted that he liked you too much to be a real jerk to you." He smiles wistfully. "I knew you cared about me, Gretchen. I did think you loved me, honestly, but that you just didn't know it. How's that for being an arrogant fool? But I really thought we were going to end up together. I thought I just had to wait till you realized I was who you were meant to be with.

"I didn't count on you meeting someone like Joe. The minute you introduced us, I knew I'd badly miscalculated. And there wasn't a damn thing I could do about it. I mean, I did try. I told you when we said goodbye that night that there was something I wanted to talk to you about. I planned to call you the next day and tell you I loved you. But you called me first and left me that voicemail. Said you were engaged to be married. I mean, you told me that in a voicemail!"

Why did I do that? I suddenly wonder. Why did I not tell him in person? Did I leave him a voicemail because I was afraid that hearing his warm, familiar voice on the phone might make me doubt my decision to marry Joe? But I truly didn't think Vic cared about me that way. Or did I wonder? Oh, I don't know!

We stare at each other. Then he walks over and leans against the car beside me, drumming his fingers lightly against the metal.

"You could have stayed friends with me," I whisper.

He shakes his head. "I'm sorry. I couldn't do that. I just couldn't do it, Gretchen."

"You broke my heart," I say.

"Yeah? Well, you broke my heart, too."

We look out on the lawn together. His dad still grows blueberries, an enormous field of them. I used to come out here and pick them with Vic.

"When did you decide to come to the reunion?" I ask.

"Two days ago," he says.

"After I signed up?"

"Yes."

"You booked a flight from Seattle two days ago to be here in Upstate New York last night?"

"Yes."

"Was it a direct flight?"

He shakes his head. "No. Three different planes. It cost a small fortune, too."

We stand for a while in silence, listening to chirping crickets and watching a hummingbird drink from a nearby feeder.

"Will you promise me something?" I ask.

"What?" he says.

"Don't disappear on me again. Can you promise me that?"

He's silent for a moment. I look at him and then follow his gaze out over the blueberry fields.

"Can you promise me something?" Vic asks.

"What?" I ask.

"Don't marry someone else. Can you promise me that?"

I want to laugh, and I also feel tears brimming in my eyes again. I blink them away. Does he mean what I think he means? Is he that sure about me? Am I that sure about him? Is such a thing even possible after all these years?

My stomach clenches. I can't let him get away again. I can't lose him again. Yes, I am that sure. "Yes, Vic, I can promise you that."

He turns to face me, his eyes soft, a smile teasing the corner of his lips. "You know something?" he says. "It's possible I've been in love with you since the fourth grade."

I'm smiling so wide my cheeks hurt. He brushes his knuckles against my knuckles. I spread my fingers, and he intertwines his fingers with mine. His hand is strong, warm. I squeeze and Vic squeezes back.

He clears his throat. "It turns out that about thirty years ago I made a really, really stupid mistake," he says. "I don't regret the life I've lived. I don't. And I'm happy for you for the good things you've had in your life. But I'm wondering, Gretchen, if I can have that prom kiss now."

"You told me to never try to kiss you again, and I promised myself I wouldn't," I whisper.

"Please, please break that promise," he whispers back.

I wrap my arms around his waist and lift my face up to his. His arms circle my back. He pulls me close and lowers his face to mine. And we kiss.

ACKNOWLEDGMENTS

Many thanks to my parents for raising me in a household filled with books, and to my mother for taking me and my brothers on frequent trips to local public libraries. That's where my love of stories began.

Thanks to my brothers and first readers, Dave and Nat, for your brutal honesty, insightful suggestions, and unflagging encouragement. You have made this writing journey so much more enjoyable because I always know I'll have at least two readers for every draft of every story. Any success I ever have in my writing career will be thanks to you.

My second cousin, Elisabeth Stevens, wrote fiction for decades: short stories and novels, which she published with a small press. Not only was she an inspiring role model of a writer persevering and believing in herself, but she read drafts of some of my early stories and encouraged me to keep writing, enjoy the process, and never stop developing my craft. Someone told me once, when I fretted that I might die before I read *War and Peace*: "If in my Father's house there are many rooms, one of them must be a library." Betsy, I hope this little book of stories makes it into that library. I'd love to have you read it.

When I started writing fiction, I thought I would want to be traditionally published, so that all I would have to do is write, and someone else would take care of everything else. Well, it's no longer true even for traditionally published authors that someone else is taking care of everything else. All writers today need to figure out branding and marketing and how to find their readers. I thought I would hate all that, but I don't. Yes, the indie-publishing process is challenging, but to my surprise, I'm finding it lots of fun.

So much of that fun has to do with the team I've been able to put together. Thank you, Vasheena Brisbane and Brisbane Creative LLC, for your strategizing insights, website design and tech support, and your positive, patient, "it will happen" attitude.

Nancy Brandwein, I'm so glad I met you on vacation. Somehow, I made it through an entire MFA program without ever hearing of the concept of a developmental editor. What a difference it has made to have your eyes on my story structure. I appreciate your critical feedback about the stories that aren't ready yet, and your stamp of approval on these five.

Juliet Pritner, thank you for copyediting all these stories, and narrating the audiobook for *Pinkie*. It's been amazing to hear your artistic interpretation of my story. Hoping the stars align so we can do it again!

To Karen, my talented and generous sister-in-law, thank you for all your meticulous work formatting the print books. You are amazing and I couldn't have done it without you.

My cousin Laura, thank you for your editorial and artistic eye. I'm always so grateful for your ideas and wisdom about the writing process and publishing journey.

Thank you, Maryna at MaryDes, for the lovely cover designs for these five stories.

To my RWA-NYC critique group, it has been so rewarding to

walk beside you on your writing journeys and to have you walk alongside me.

To my beta readers, for the gift of your time and your incredibly helpful feedback on my works in progress, I cannot thank you enough.

More friends than I can possibly name have listened to me talk about my writing dreams, read drafts of stories, and encouraged me on this journey. I won the friend lottery and I'm so grateful.

To my husband, Jim, and our children, Cullen and Lucy, thank you for your love, encouragement, and support. It means the world. I can't wait to give you the first copies of my first book.

And finally, thank you to my readers, not only for reading these stories, but for your emails and reviews. I can't tell you how much your personal messages and encouraging comments have meant to me, especially your interest in reading longer works from me. I promise, I'm hard at work on a novel (or three or five) and your kind words offer me motivation and inspiration. I appreciate you so much.

A WORD ABOUT THE TITLE

Spend enough time reading romances, and you will find writers paying homage, subtle and not-so-subtle, to Jane Austen, author of the quintessential romance, *Pride and Prejudice.* The title of this book, *First Impressions: Five Short Love Stories,* is my not-so-subtle homage to a writer who has brought me decades of delight.

ABOUT THE AUTHOR

KATE COURTRIGHT has found joy in stories her entire life. A romantic at heart, she loves reading and writing stories that make her laugh and cry and believe in the power of love to change people's lives. Kate wrote her first story, about Cinderella eating spaghetti, when she was seven years old and has been writing in one form or another ever since. She lives with her family in New York City and enjoys escaping to small towns and inviting bodies of water whenever she can.

Go to www.katecourtright.com to sign up for her bi-monthly newsletter and reach her by email at: kate@katecourtright.com.

The more reviews a book has, the more readers will discover it. Every review helps, even just a sentence or two. If you enjoyed *First Impressions: Five Short Love Stories*, please consider leaving an online review on the platforms of your choice and know that the author will be very grateful.

Printed in Great Britain
by Amazon

20442478R00128